NORSE MYTHS

with love and admiration – K. C-H.

For Gwyneth and Arthur – J. A. L.

For Will Wareing.

NORSE MYTHS

Tales of Odin, Thor and Loki

in new versions by **Kevin Crossley-Holland**

illustrated by **Jeffrey Alan Love**

WALKER STUDIO

AN IMPRINT OF WALKER BOOKS

FOREWORD

What are the Norse myths, exactly? Well, the Vikings believed that human beings inhabited Middle Earth, and shared it with greedy dwarfs who lived in gloomy caves and rock crevices, and powerful giants who lived in the mountains away across the sea – an ocean that, like a shimmering bracelet, encircled their whole world.

Above Middle Earth, or Midgard, lived the gods in their green-and-gold realm of Asgard, and below Midgard was the third level, the world of the dead, ruled over by a woman whose body was half alive and half a corpse. The axis of these three levels was a colossal ash tree, Yggdrasill. Everything alive depended on it and fed off it, and the Vikings called it their Guardian Tree, their Suffering Tree, their Tree of Life.

As the Vikings became Christian, they slowly turned away from their old beliefs, and their worship of gods and goddesses of the weather and the sea and everything that grows on earth and good health and justice and good luck. This is when a man living in Iceland wrote down these myths – with a quill and ink and parchment – because he feared that they might be forgotten. He lived eight hundred years ago and his name was Snorri Sturluson.

When I first read these stories as a boy, I yelled and laughed and cried a little, and knew myself a bit better.

The Norse myths are brilliant, fast-moving, ice-bright stories. The first tells how the world was created and the last is an incredible description of how it will be destroyed – only to begin again. And in between, we are caught up in the see-sawing battle for power between the gods and the giants, a struggle punctuated by surprising love-matches, riddle-duels, thrilling journeys, thefts and recoveries, running and eating and drinking and wrestling contests, and dazzling magic.

Odin (known as Allfather) is chief of gods, the god of poetry, battle and death. His son is mighty Thor, god of thunder, law and order. They give their names to our Wednesday (Odin's Day) and Thursday (Thor's Day). Without the protection of Thor and his short-handled hammer, the gods wouldn't be able to keep the giants at bay for very long. Freyr and his beautiful sister Freyja are both fertility gods. Freyr is responsible for the growth and ripening of crops and Freyja cares for the conception and birth of babies. The god Njord controls the oceans and the winds, and the goddess Idun looks after the apples of youth. In all, there are thirteen gods and thirteen goddesses.

Terrifying as the giants are, the greatest enemy of the gods is one of their own number, Loki. Sly and slippery and fast-talking and shape-changing, Loki is a trickster – and to begin with he is no more than a nuisance. But as time passes, his own jealousy and spite and fury darken him. He causes the death of the best and most beautiful of the gods, Balder; and in the last terrible battle (he sails to it in a boat made of fingernails), he sides with the evil giants and monsters.

In the myths, the gods and supernatural beings are really exaggerations of the Vikings who created and worshipped them. They try to explain how humans are as we are, and how things came to be. They tell us about ourselves and our world not as modern scientists would, but through the lens of imaginative story-telling, coloured by the beauty and expanse and extremes of the icy, fiery landscape where they originated.

When I think about the Vikings or talk about the Vikings my eyes brighten, my heart beats faster, and sometimes my hair stands on end. Energetic and practical and witty and daring and quarrelsome and passionate, always eager to go to the edge and see and find out more: that's how Vikings were. Their tough and stubborn and often beautiful women managed self-sufficient farmsteads in Norway and Sweden and Denmark and Iceland and Greenland, and were at least as capable and outspoken as their men. And for around three centuries – from the beginning of the ninth to the end of the eleventh – many of their husbands and not a few of their sons and daughters sailed south and east and west in their elegant and superbly made clinker boats as mercenaries, traders, hit-and-run raiders, settlers and rulers. And of course they took their gods and beliefs and language with them.

Snorri Sturluson! If you'd been able to ask him whether or not these stories were true, he might have replied, "Well, I think it's best to believe nothing and everything, in a way." And what he did actually write was this: "Well, now, I've never heard of anyone who has written down more about the story of the world!"

Kevin Crossley-Holland
Chalk Hill, November 2017

5

THE MYTHS

Some men and women become great, and the giants are certainly strong, but the gods and goddesses are even stronger and greater.

GODS AND GODDESSES

Odin: the ruler of the gods; known as Allfather;

the god of battle and poetry

Loki: the son of two giants;

a mischief-making trickster

Thor: the god of thunder; son of Odin;

fights with his hammer Mjollnir

Freyr: the god of plenty
and the Sun; brother
to Freyja

Frigg: the foremost of
the goddesses; the wife of
Odin and mother of Balder

Balder: the best and
most gentle of the gods;
Odin and Frigg's son

Hod: Balder's
blind brother

Freyja: the most beautiful
of all the goddesses;
Freyr's sister

Njord: the god of
seafarers and fishermen

Sif: Thor's
golden-haired wife

Heimdall: the watchman
of the gods

Idun: the keeper of
the golden apples of youth

DWARFS AND GIANTS

Fjalar and Galar: brew the

mead of poetry; brothers

Son One and Son Two:

skilled smiths; sons of Ivaldi

Brokk and Eitri:

skilled smiths; brothers

Alvis: knowledgeable

about the nine worlds

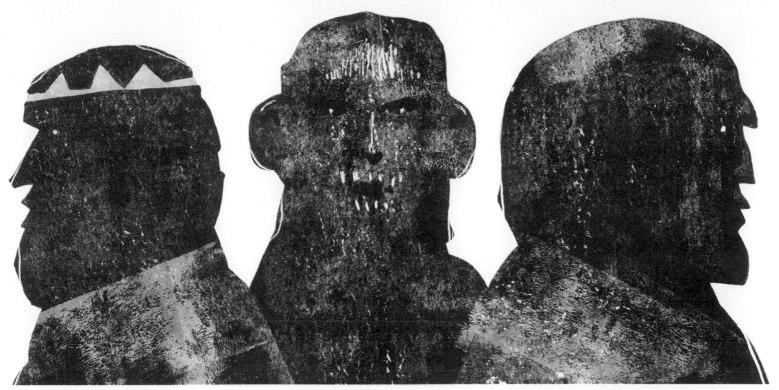

The Giant King: lives in Utgard, a great fortress in Jotunheim

Hrungnir: strongest of all the giants

Geirrod: hates the gods

Suttung: keeper of the mead of poetry

Gerd: renowned for her ravishing beauty

Thiazi and Skadi: father and daughter; known for skiing and hunting

THE NORSE WORLD

YGGDRASILL

The great ash tree YGGDRASILL links the nine worlds of Norse mythology. It has three roots, each connected to a different level of the universe. The first root is bedded in ASGARD, home of the gods and goddesses. The second root sinks into MIDGARD, home of the humans and dwarfs, and JOTUNHEIM, realm of the giants. Midgard is connected to Asgard by BIFROST, a three-strand rainbow bridge, and encircled by a giant serpent, JORMUNGAND. Yggdrasill's third root reaches far down into NIFLHEIM, the world of the dead.

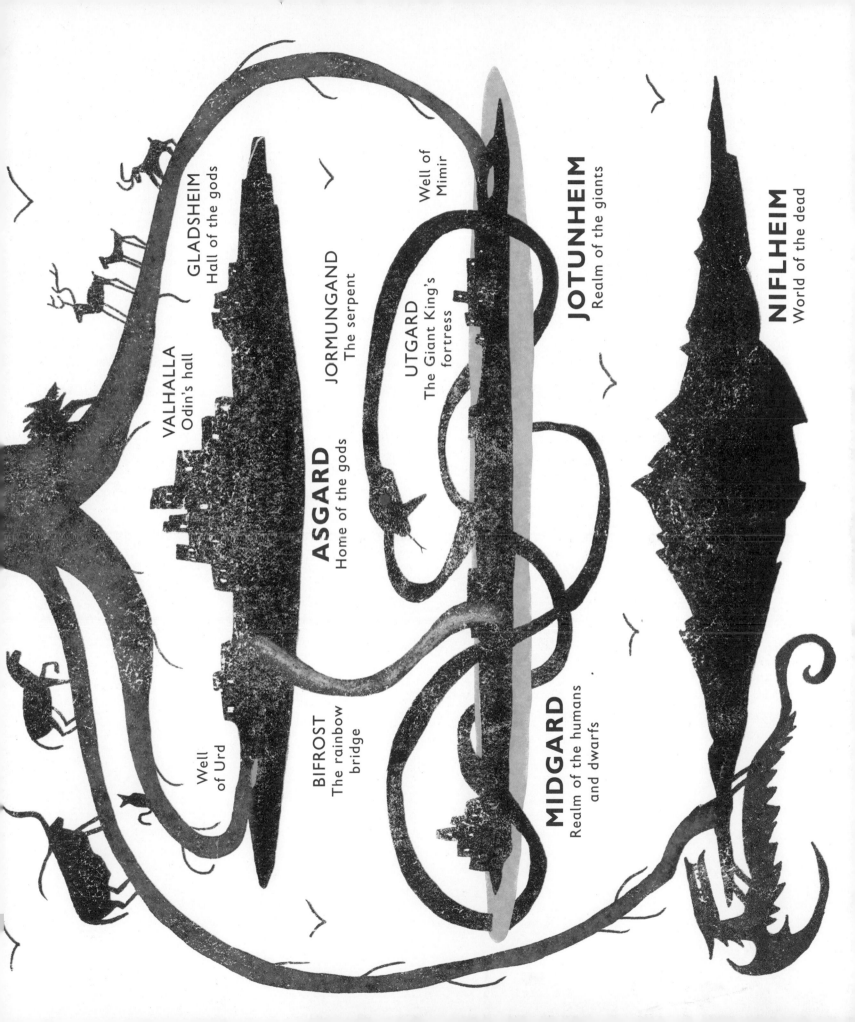

VALHALLA
Odin's hall

GLADSHEIM
Hall of the gods

Well
of Urd

ASGARD
Home of the gods

JORMUNGAND
The serpent

Well of
Mimir

BIFROST
The rainbow
bridge

UTGARD
The Giant King's
fortress

JOTUNHEIM
Realm of the giants

MIDGARD
Realm of the humans
and dwarfs

NIFLHEIM
World of the dead

IN THE BEGINNING

Be generous, be spirited,

and you'll lead a happy life.

There was a King of Sweden called Gylfi. He knew a great deal more than most men and women because he listened to story-tellers, and because he was curious and had a good memory.

He knew that there were nine worlds and that these worlds were on three levels – rather like three huge platters suspended one above the other, with an enormous space between each of them. He knew the top level was called Asgard, and the middle one was Midgard and the bottom one was a dark world called Niflheim.

King Gylfi knew that Asgard was where the gods and god-desses lived and that, unless you could fly like an eagle or a falcon or maybe a lark, the only way you could get there from Sweden was to cross the swaying road, the three-strand rainbow bridge, Bifrost. He knew that human beings and all kinds of animals and birds shared the middle level with the frost-giants and rock-giants who lived far away to the north, and with dwarfs who lived in potholes and caves and rock fissures. And Gylfi had heard that dead men and women lived in the freezing underworld of Niflheim, a hard ride nine days and nine nights downward from Midgard.

Not only this — King Gylfi had actually met one of the goddesses without realizing it. This is what happened.

Sometimes in spring and summer, the king disguised himself, so that no one would recognize him, and rode or walked around Sweden to see the country he loved so much, meet a few of his subjects and add to his hoard of knowledge.

"These are my quests," he used to say to himself, "my quests for songs and stories and secrets."

One spring morning, the king overtook a beggar-woman, who looked as if she were on her last legs. True, she was wearing a mustard-and-blue bandanna and had a friendly, toothless smile, but it was all she could do to stay steady on her feet.

"I'm all right," she told the king, "but as dry as a bulrush. I'm just on my way to the well over there."

So King Gylfi helped her along, and when they had reached the well, not far from a longhouse, he drew up a clanking bucket of fresh water.

The owner of the nearby longhouse had left

a wooden mug on the coping of the well for the use of travellers, and the beggar-woman courteously insisted that Gylfi should drink first.

"Wait!" she said, and she stooped and picked several scented violets and dropped the petals into the mug.

Not only that. With shaking hands, the beggar-woman loosened the little sack tied around her waist and pulled out a small wedge of crumbly pale cheese and a couple of rather shrivelled apples.

"Beggars can't be choosers," she said with a tight little smile. "They still taste good."

"Yes," said the king. "And it's April. Cuckoo month. The very best time to set off on journeys."

"Where are you going?" the beggar-woman asked him.

Gylfi shook his head. "I never know until I get there," he replied.

The beggar-woman sniffed.

"I'll tell you this," said Gylfi. "You've drawn fresh water and scented it with violets and asked me to drink first. You've shared with me the few scraps you have. So now it's my turn to do you a good deed."

Gylfi spread his arms as wide as the kingdom of Sweden, and filled his lungs with cool air, and smiled. "Is there anywhere in Midgard as beautiful as this?" he asked. "And I'm going

to give you as much of this land as a team of four oxen is able to plough in one day and one night."

The beggar-woman's eyes shone as silver as the blebs of melting icicles.

The king couldn't tell what the beggar-woman was thinking. And he had no idea that she too was in disguise. She was the goddess Gefion.

For a while the king and the beggar-woman padded along together, but when they came to a place where four green roads met, they parted company. Gylfi went west but the goddess walked north and hurried all the way across Midgard to Jotunheim, the realm of the giants. She waded across the shallow, rapid river known as the Elivagar and tramped on until she reached the farm in the mountains. That's where her four sons lived, and they were the sons of a giant.

"I've got a job for you," their mother told her sons and, using magical words, she changed them into four massive oxen. And when they bellowed, they made such a noise that you would have thought they were trying to raise the floor of Asgard.

The goddess harnessed the oxen and led them straight back across the Elivagar and then through Sweden to a shining green plain. There she yoked them to a plough with a large coulter, and put them to work.

"Pull!" Gefion urged her sons. "Pull! Pull!"

The four oxen pulled and grunted and pulled. They slipped, they slid, they reeked of sweat. And after one day and one night, they had dragged the whole beautiful plain – the grass, the soft earth in which it was bedded, the plain's deep footing of clay and flint – far away to the west, right into the shallow sea.

The goddess Gefion told her four sons to halt. She unyoked them, and the crust of land they had dragged there settled into the water, and formed a luscious island, firm and springy underfoot.

Gefion called this island Zeeland, and that is how it was created.

From the streams all around, and from below, and from above too when the clouds wept to see how the oxen had torn away the green plain, fresh water seeped and dripped into the earth's wide wound. So the wound slowly became a lake, and the people nearby called it Mälar. And that's why the shape of Zeeland fits into the bays and bights of Lake Mälar.

When he saw what had happened, King Gylfi was shocked. Not only did his people of Sweden depend on all the oats and wheat grown on the fertile plain, but he realized that his own great generosity had been repaid with a trick. In return for his kindness, the old beggar-woman wearing a mustard-and-blue bandanna had looted his land.

Much as the king knew, because he listened to storytellers and was curious, and had a good memory, he realized that he needed to find out a great deal more about the gods and goddesses and the realm of Asgard. "Why," he said to himself, "I didn't even know that they can be as cunning and deceitful as human beings."

I know how life began, he thought. I've heard how a region of fog and blue ice drifted south, and how a region of blazing fire, guarded by the black giant Surt, spread north until the two regions met in the enormous emptiness called Ginnungagap.

Then orange-and-golden flames began to melt the ice, and licked it into the shape of a terrifying frost-giant called Ymir.

Those mountains over there, Gylfi thought, between Sweden and Norway, they're made from Ymir's bones. The sea was made from his blood and the sky from his skull, and his brains are the clouds. In fact, the whole of the nine worlds are made from Ymir's body.

Yes, I've heard the first gods were Odin and his two brothers, Vili and Ve, and they were actually the sons of a giantess. One day they were walking along the foreshore when they came across a fallen elm tree and a fallen ash tree. Odin raised the two bedraggled trees and breathed the spirit of life into them, and then Vili offered them keen wits and feeling hearts, and Ve gave them the gifts of hearing and smell and speech. So everyone in Midgard is descended from those three gods.

But much as I know, thought the king, I still know so little. I want to find out more about the other gods and goddesses, especially Thor, the god of thunder, and how he fights against the giants.

The trickster Loki too! I want to know more about him and his practical jokes.

■ ■ ■

So in that same spring season, King Gylfi set off alone from Sweden. After walking for seven days through sweet-smelling woodlands of pine and silver birch, and sleeping in old barns, he reached the foot of the swaying rainbow bridge, Bifrost.

Before the king stepped onto the bridge, he decided to disguise himself because he had no idea what awaited him.

He crouched and murmured magic sounds and meanings so softly that not even the gossiping wind could hear him. He changed himself into a stumbling, fumbling tramp.

"I'll call myself Gangleri," he said. "Gangleri, yes. Footsore."

Before Gangleri had reached the other side of the bridge, Heimdall, watchman of the gods, whose eyesight was so keen that he could spot a seal swimming in the ocean hundreds of miles away, blew a blast on his horn to warn the gods and goddesses that they had a visitor.

"I've walked up from Midgard,"

Gangleri told Heimdall, "and it's further than far. Will I be welcome here?"

"That depends on why you've come," Heimdall replied.

"To find out."

"Find out?"

"Yes," said Gangleri seriously. "Everything."

Heimdall smiled, and Gangleri saw that all his teeth were made of gold. "Enter," said the god. "Go under that gateway, and follow the wide path beyond it. You'll come to a huge meeting-place, a hall with a roof made of overlapping gold shields. It belongs to our ruler, Odin."

At the entrance to the courtyard of this hall a man was juggling with seven glittering knives.

"Who are you?" the juggler called out.

"Gangleri. I've tramped all the way from Midgard."

"Never been there," said the juggler, without taking his eyes off his knives for one moment.

"It's further than far," Gangleri told him. "Will I be welcome here?"

"Whoever comes in peace is welcome," the juggler said. "Not that living men or women often come this far."

"What is this place, anyhow?" Gangleri asked. "It looks ten times as large as the palace of the King of Sweden."

"It's Valhalla," the juggler replied. "I'll take you in."

Still juggling, the man led Gangleri into a vast, rather smoky hall, and courteously stood aside so that the guest could lead the way. And even though he hadn't closed it, the king heard the door slam shut by itself.

Gangleri passed men sitting at long tables, playing chess and draughts and other board games, drinking mugs of ale, elbow-wrestling, and beyond them were pairs of men wrestling and practising sword-play. The king rubbed the smoke out of his eyes but as he turned to ask the juggler who they all were, he saw at the far end of the hall a most extraordinary sight: not one but three high seats, each placed above the other, and each with a bearded figure sitting on it.

"Who are they?" Gangleri asked the juggler.

"Three wise kings," the juggler said. "They are not as great as the gods but they're greater than humans."

Gangleri looked puzzled. "Where do they come from?"

21

"I cannot say," replied the juggler. "The wise ruler in the lowest seat is called High One."

"High One?"

"The middle one is Just-as-High… And the top one is Third."

"Third!" replied Gangleri, frowning and smiling and shaking his head, all at the same time.

"You could say that they are one-in-three or that they're three-in-one, depending on how you look at it," said the juggler. He laughed and, still juggling, turned his back on Gangleri and walked out of the hall.

"I don't know what you mean," Gangleri said to himself. "What's the difference?"

Then Gangleri picked his way up the hall, and the three wise kings gazed down at him.

"Whoever you are," High One said, "you are welcome to eat and drink with us."

"Gladly," said Gangleri. "I've come from further than far."

"Further than far," High One repeated. "Why? What do you want?"

"Answers," replied Gangleri. "Even before I eat or drink, I must have answers, but my questions aren't easy ones. Is there anyone up here likely to be able to answer them?"

"You've come to the right place," High One told him. "If we can't answer them, no one can. Step forward please."

"I know there are nine worlds on three levels," Gangleri began, "and I know the gods and goddesses live in Asgard. But can you tell me: who is the foremost of all the gods?"

"Allfather," said Just-as-High. "Odin, the god of inspiration, god of magic, god of brave warriors. He and his brothers Vili and Ve created man and woman from two fallen trees they found on the foreshore between the round earth and the ring of the sea. Serve Odin as children serve their fathers."

"For nine nights he hung on the great ash tree Yggdrasill to win knowledge of the magic runes; and at the Well of Mimir he sacrificed one eye to win yet greater wisdom," High One added.

"Odin, yes," rumbled Third from the topmost seat. "But he has one hundred other names. The Terrible One and Shouter and Spear Shaker, Flame-Eyed and Deep Hood, Death Blinder and Magician and—"

"That's a devil of a lot of names." Gangleri interrupted him. "Who are the other chief gods?"

"Very long ago," Just-as-High replied, "there were wars in Asgard between the Warrior Gods and the gods who safeguard green growth and harvest here and all over Midgard. We call them the Green-and-Gold Gods. In the end, all the gods made a truce, and so our chief gods come from both sides."

"Thor, the son of Odin, he's a Warrior God—" High One began.

"I've heard of him," Gangleri said. "Everyone has. The thunder god. People say that, without him and his hammer Mjollnir, the giants would attack and conquer Asgard."

"He's certainly one of the chief gods," High One continued, "and so is Freyr, the leader of the Green-and-Gold Gods, and his beautiful sister Freyja."

"Who was Odin's wife, then?" Gangleri asked.

"Frigg," said High One. "She is foremost of all the goddesses, and the mother of the best and most gentle of the gods, Balder."

"Yes," Just-as-High agreed, "and Bragi is the god of poetry and eloquence, and Eir is the goddess of healing, and there are gods of bravery and justice, and goddesses of love and marriage and—"

"How many gods and goddesses are there, then?" asked Gangleri.

"Thirteen gods and thirteen goddesses," High One replied.

Third cleared his throat. "Not forgetting Loki," he said in his deep voice.

"Yes, I've heard of him too, and how he plays practical jokes, and makes everyone laugh," Gangleri said.

"Loki is not altogether a god," Third explained. "He's the son of the giant Farbauti, but he lives with the gods. He can shape-shift and make himself as small as a fly, and it's true that he used to make everyone laugh."

"For a long time," Just-as-High said, "Loki kept getting the gods into trouble, but he always helped them out of it."

"But that has changed," said Third in a low voice. "Loki has changed. He has become bitter and cruel. He is the enemy of the gods and they have imprisoned him."

■ ■ ■

For a while the three wise kings sat in silence and King Gylfi, disguised as a tramp called Gangleri, stood in silence.

Then High One showed his palms to Gangleri. "You are welcome to eat and drink with us," he said.

"Gladly," said Gangleri. "But first! You said the gods and goddesses shape and guide the lives of human beings in Midgard…"

"They do," agreed High One.

"But are they friendly with some of the giants too? And with dwarfs? And the elves? And what about the dead?"

Just-as-High sighed. "Have you ever heard anyone ask so many questions?" he said.

"Some giants we call rock-giants," High One explained, "and some we call frost-giants, and they're all as bad as each other. Brutes! Numbskulls!"

"What they want is to destroy all the gods and goddesses," Just-as-High added.

"And yet—" rumbled Third.

"I was coming to that," Just-as-High interrupted him. "A few gods and giants have made friendships and even fallen in love."

"Have you heard of the goddess Gefion?" High One asked.

"Gefion, yes, Gefion," he mumbled.

"She has four sons, and their father's a giant."

"Blunt as bludgeons," Just-as-High went on. "That's what giants are. Brutal! But the dwarfs..."

"No dwarf ever does anything for anyone else," High One told Gangleri. "Not even another dwarf. They're lustful and grasping and greedy – especially for gold."

"Not every god is wholly good," Third explained. "And not every giant or dwarf is wholly bad. Think of who you are at your best, Gangleri. That's when you're most godlike; now think of who you are at your worst. That's when you're most like giants and dwarfs. That's when..."

Third's last words were drowned by a clang and clatter in the body of the great hall Valhalla. Gangleri turned round and saw that dozens of men had got to their feet, shouting, and were overturning benches. Then they bunched into a scrum, shouting and fighting.

Third stood up in his high seat. He raised his right hand. And almost as suddenly as the uproar had broken out, it began to subside.

"These men are heroes," Third told Gangleri. "When they were killed on a battlefield in Midgard, they were chosen to live again here in Valhalla."

"Chosen?" asked Gangleri. "Who chooses them?"

"Odin's beautiful young women, the Valkyries. They bring the bravest warriors back here to Valhalla."

"And before long," High One said, "Odin will need them."

"Here and now," Just-as-High said, "they're angry and upset because they're so hungry and thirsty. They can't begin to eat or drink, though – not before any guest in this hall has begun to eat."

"Ah!" exclaimed Gangleri, shaking his head. "In that case ... I must ask you later..."

"We've already told you more wonders than we've ever told any other human being," High One announced. "We'll tell you no more."

Gangleri lowered his eyes. "Just one last question," he pleaded. "I've heard

there's a World Tree? The great ash tree Yggdrasill."

"No one can say when it was a seed and a sapling," Just-as-High replied, "but we know it has three roots, one here in Asgard, one in the world of the giants and one in Niflheim, the realm of the dead."

"We call it the World Tree and the Guardian Tree," High One said, "because its branches spread over all the nine worlds, and it cares for us and guards us all."

"As we have explained," said Third, "Allfather hung from that tree for nine nights. And when he came back to Asgard, he told the gods: 'I hung from the windswept tree, the gallows tree. My side was pierced with a spear. I was a sacrifice to Odin, myself to myself.'"

Gangleri shook his head in wonder.

"And he told the gods," Third added, "that he had learned eighteen magic runes."

"All the gods meet beside the top-most root of Yggdrasill," Just-as-High continued. "They meet there each day and consult with the Three Norns, the three women who decide when each human being will be born and what will happen in their lives and when they must die."

"Must whatever begins also end?" asked Gangleri.

All at the same time, the three wise kings stood up, and stared down at Gangleri.

"Now you know more than anyone else in Midgard," they pronounced, and Gangleri realized that all three of them were speaking in unison, as if they were one voice – one-in-three and three-in-one.

"More than anyone else in Midgard," the three kings repeated, "and you must share it. Not only this. All around you in Sweden, and throughout the northern world, there are stories about the gods and goddesses. Give your life to seeking. Invite people to your court to tell them, and ask your scribes to write them down, so that men and women and children will never forget them. You must share them all…"

But then Gangleri heard a grinding and a roaring, as if the walls of Valhalla were collapsing. He put his hands over his head, hunched his shoulders and screwed up his eyes…

And when he opened them again, King Gylfi was standing back in Sweden, in the open air, alone and surrounded by a sea of waving grasses and bobbing wildflowers, buttery gold and kingfisher-blue and scarlet.

There was no hall. No juggler. No mysterious wise kings.

Nothing but a story and a beginning.

THE WALL OF ASGARD

Fair words often conceal weaselly thinking.

Which matters more? Mastery of the skills of warfare or mastery of the skills of farming and fishing?

No sooner had the gods built their halls in Asgard than they began to argue. Then they began to fight. Long before King Gylfi had walked up over the rainbow bridge, the Green-and-Gold Gods of fair weather and good harvests, led by Freyr and his father Njord and his sister Freyja, fought against the Warrior Gods led by Odin the Allfather and his son Thor.

This was the first war in the world,

and when neither side was able to win, the Warrior Gods and the Green-and-Gold Gods felt drained and exhausted. The one thing they agreed on was that anything, anything at all, would be better than more conflict. And so they engaged in almost unending undertakings, under-standings, bargaining. A war of words.

When the gods looked around them, they saw that most of their great meeting-places had been wrecked. The hall with pillars of red gold ... the hall so high it looked like a cliff ... the hall made of overlapping planks like a boat ... the hall Sokkvabekk that was surrounded by water and had a sinking floor. Even Valhalla, the hall with five hundred and forty doors, thatched with spears and shields, where Odin gathered slain war-riors around him, had been shattered.

"Unless we make peace with one another," Odin said, "how can we hope to guard ourselves against our true enemies, the giants?"

Allfather pointed at the ruins of the vast wall that had once surrounded Asgard. Jagged. Gat-toothed. Grassy. He waved at all the huge blocks of roughly dressed stone scattered in the fields where cattle grazed.

"First things first," Odin said. "We must rebuild the wall that surrounds us all. Whatever men build, they soon de-stroy or abandon. But what we build, Warrior Gods and Green-and-Gold Gods together, shoulder to shoulder, will grow from the cornerstone of peace, and guard us against our enemies for ever."

"Who will be our master-builder?" his wife Frigg asked. "Which one of us?"

"I can make crops to grow and ripen," said Freyr, leader of the Green-and-Gold Gods, "but I can't grow walls."

"I'm no builder," said Idun, keeper of the golden apples of youth, "but I'll give each and every craftsman an apple each day so that they're just as young when they finish building the wall as on the day they begin it."

"We're not unwilling," said Thor's wife, golden-haired Sif. "We know how much we need a wall to guard us against the giants and whatever is dark and dreadful in the lower worlds. But we're not master-builders. Not one of us can do this."

"Not even I can rebuild it!" exclaimed Thor.

"Your mouths are full of nothing," Odin told them. "Nothing but *can't* and *won't*."

Some of the gods peered into the pale blue skull of the sky; some stared at their feet.

"Well then, Odin," drawled Loki, the shape-shifter. His eyes flickered and he batted his long orange eyelashes. "What's your idea? Tell us your plan."

Odin glared at him.

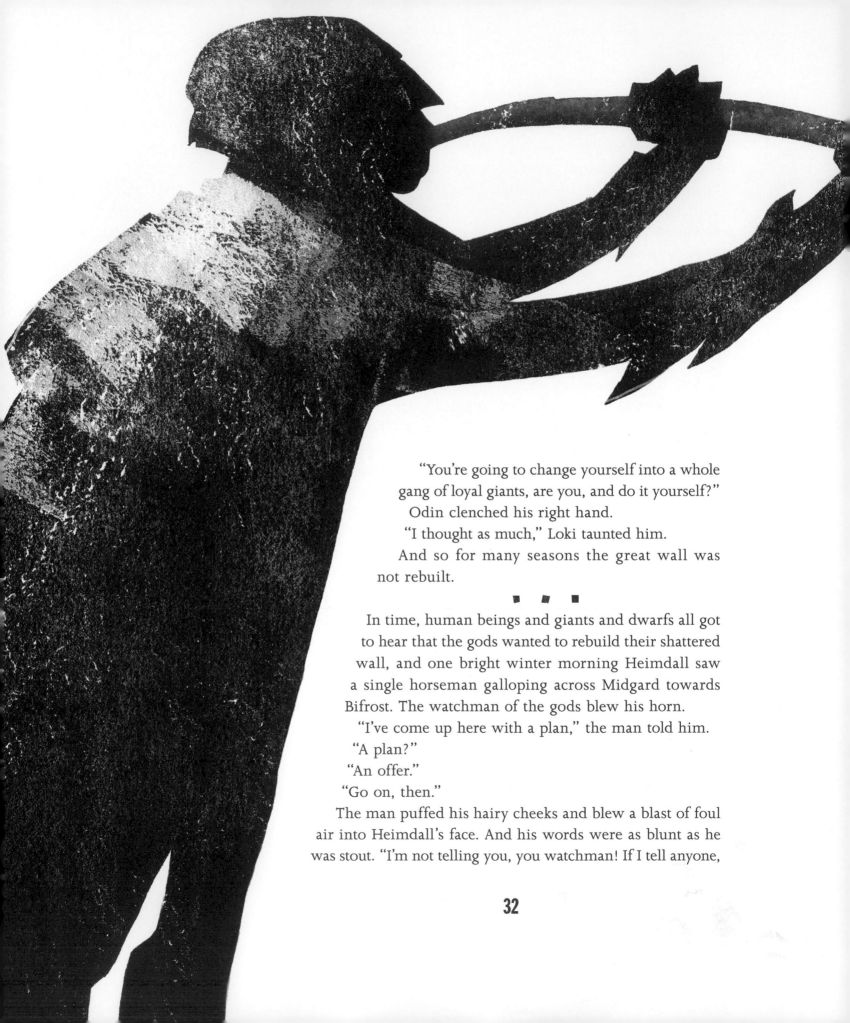

"You're going to change yourself into a whole gang of loyal giants, are you, and do it yourself?"

Odin clenched his right hand.

"I thought as much," Loki taunted him.

And so for many seasons the great wall was not rebuilt.

■ ◾ ■

In time, human beings and giants and dwarfs all got to hear that the gods wanted to rebuild their shattered wall, and one bright winter morning Heimdall saw a single horseman galloping across Midgard towards Bifrost. The watchman of the gods blew his horn.

"I've come up here with a plan," the man told him.

"A plan?"

"An offer."

"Go on, then."

The man puffed his hairy cheeks and blew a blast of foul air into Heimdall's face. And his words were as blunt as he was stout. "I'm not telling you, you watchman! If I tell anyone,

32

I'll tell everyone. Call them together."

"Not Thor," said Heimdall. "He's been away for many weeks, fighting giants. Getting rid of them before they trouble us."

"All the others, then," said the horseman, and he sounded so sure of himself that Heimdall blew his horn for a second time and waved him towards the gritty track leading through a wrecked gateway to the Plain of Ida and the great hall Gladsheim, Place of Joy.

All the gods and goddesses trooped across the plain where sheep strayed and cattle grazed. They assembled in the ruins of Gladsheim, and one-eyed Allfather stared at the horseman and signalled to him to dismount.

"Your message?" he asked.

The horseman shook his head. "No, not a message," he replied slowly.

"What, then?"

"I've heard you're looking for someone to rebuild your wall."

"A team," said Odin. "Hired hands. A gang. An army."

"I'll do it. I'll rebuild it."

As when a small wind all at once gets up from nowhere, there was a stirring in Gladsheim.

"So you're a mason, are you?" Odin said. "A master-builder."

"And it will be a good deal thicker and higher than it was to begin with," the horseman said. "You won't have to worry yourselves about rock-giants or frost-giants or anything else."

"Not even the dragon?" asked Sif.

"Certainly not," the horseman said. "He devours black corpses, not golden-haired goddesses."

"The gods have a saying—" Odin began.

But the horseman rudely interrupted him. "Eighteen months," he announced.

"Eighteen," repeated Odin. "And what's your price?"

The horseman pushed out his thick lower lip, and nodded. "My price?" he repeated quite casually, as if he were asking for hay for his horse. "The most beautiful of all your beauties. Freyja! The goddess Freyja."

"Never!" shouted Odin.

"You heard me. Freyja, to be my wife."

Stout and solid as he was, the horseman was caught up and almost lifted off the ground, in a hurricane of shouting and bellowing. And sitting on a rough block of stone, Freyja froze. She sat so still that not one link in her gold choker winked. Not one gold thread in her clothing…

"Freyja," the horseman said again. "Yes, and the Sun. And the Moon. The Sun and the Moon and Freyja. That's my offer. Take it or leave it."

"How dare you?" growled Odin.

"He who dares…" leered the horseman.

"It's out of the question, and you know it," Allfather said coldly. "Go away! Go back to where you belong." And Odin swept his dark blue cloak around him and walked off.

But Loki at once put up both his hands. "Odin! Odin! Not so fast," he called out. "Few ideas are wholly good or wholly bad. We must discuss this plan. That's the least we can do, seeing as our guest has come from so far."

Odin scowled and told the horseman or mason or whoever he was to leave Gladsheim, and to take his stallion with him, while the gods discussed his offer.

"We can't possibly risk losing Freyja," Odin protested. "The goddess of love! The mistress of magic! Loki, what are you thinking of?"

"Listen!" said Loki. "We can use this man's plan…"

"Man?" said Heimdall. "Is that what he is."

"We can use it against him," said Loki. "What if we give him six months? Not eighteen but six?"

Freyja wept. Each of her tears was an almond of pure gold.

"He could never do it," Heimdall said. "Not in six months."

"Exactly," said Loki, and he grinned. "If he agrees, he'll build half our wall … and what will it cost us? Nix, nought, nothing. And if he won't agree, well, so be it."

The gods and goddesses couldn't fault Loki's idea, and yet several of them felt there was something wrong about it.

"I wish Thor was here," Odin said, slowly shaking his head. "He hasn't got much of a brain, but I'd still like to hear what he says."

As for Freyja, she could see she was being used, and she felt angry with Loki and the gods. She could scarcely believe the gods would really sacrifice her and she felt afraid.

"I dislike taking advice from a cheat and a trickster," said Odin. "However..."

Loki neighed and ran out of ruined Gladsheim and came back with the horseman and his fine stallion.

"Six months," Odin told him.

The horseman jerked his head upwards. "Impossible."

"Six months," Odin said more loudly. "Tomorrow's the winter solstice. So if you haven't finished by the summer solstice..."

"Impossible!" the man repeated. But then he gazed at the golden goddess, and he desired her so much that he began to shiver.

"Well then," said Odin.

The horseman sighed. He shook his head. "Six months," he grumbled. "In that case you must let my stallion Svadilfari help me."

The silver-grey stallion pricked up his ears.

"No," said Allfather.

"Odin, you're too stubborn," protested Loki.

"And you're too sly," Odin replied. "If I cut out your tongue, you'd find some other way of speaking."

"What can we possibly lose by letting this mason use his horse?" argued Loki. "How else can he drag up stone from the quarry?"

But Allfather was still very reluctant. "We may well come to regret this," he said.

But all the gods and goddesses agreed with the trickster – all except poor Freyja – and so Odin and the horseman swore solemn oaths, and the gods guaranteed their master-builder safe conduct and gave him and his stallion six months to build their wall.

■ ■ ■

Although Valhalla, the great meeting-hall owned by Odin, had been wrecked during the wars between the gods, the massive flight of stone steps at one end was still standing, and when Odin mounted them and sat in his high seat, Hlidskjalf, with his two ravens sitting on his shoulders, he could see everything happening in the nine worlds. But the most astonishing sight of all was right outside his own hall.

While the full Moon was sailing high, the mason led Svadilfari through the night-silence, past a little ash-copse where not a single bird was tweeting, and down to a limestone quarry so vast it would have taken an hour to run across it.

The mason took a long look at all the rocks – the teeth and jaws and broken ribs and ankle-bones of the frost-giant Ymir.

Then he spread out a coarse rope net behind Svadilfari, firmly secured it to his stallion and raised his pickaxe.

Long before the eastern sky turned rosy and the Moon's sister rose from her bed, the mason had shoved and shunted a massive pile of rock over the net, and Svadilfari had dragged it all up the slope to the gat-toothed wall.

Very early the next morning, the gods and goddesses left their own halls, or what remained of them, and walked over to where the mason was at work. They watched him smash the rocks with his sledgehammer, dress them and begin to set them in place.

Odin ground his teeth. "What did I say?" he growled.

Loki looked at the gods and goddesses, all of them silent, and he scoffed at their disquiet. "Look at you all!" he called out. And then he brayed, "Uneasy already."

"How can this mason work so fast?" muttered Odin. "Whoever he is, he's not a human being."

In the north, winter days are so short they're scarcely born before they die. But the cool spring morning when you can still see the mist-balls of your own breath brought no consolation to the gods and goddesses. They only grew more alarmed at the speed with which the mason was building their wall.

In early summer, Thor, guardian of the gods and much the strongest of them all, returned at last from his giant cull! His massacre! But none of the gods

or goddesses were much interested in hearing about it because they were so worried about the mason and Svadilfari.

Thor scratched his head. "Who swore this oath?" he asked.

"I did, of course," Odin replied.

The god of thunder frowned. "So whose idea was it?"

Odin scowled at his son. "Who do you think?"

"Not Loki!" exclaimed Thor.

■ ■ ■

the goddesses shivered. "No Sun, no Moon, each one of us in Asgard no better than a night-stumbler. Well, Loki?"

Before the trickster could reply, Freyja swept into the middle of the circle, beautiful and angry and dangerous and afraid.

"Beware!" she warned Loki in a low voice. "Those who play with fire…"

But Loki simply waved his long, pale fingers in front of her. "An oath is an oath," he replied, "and that's all there is to it."

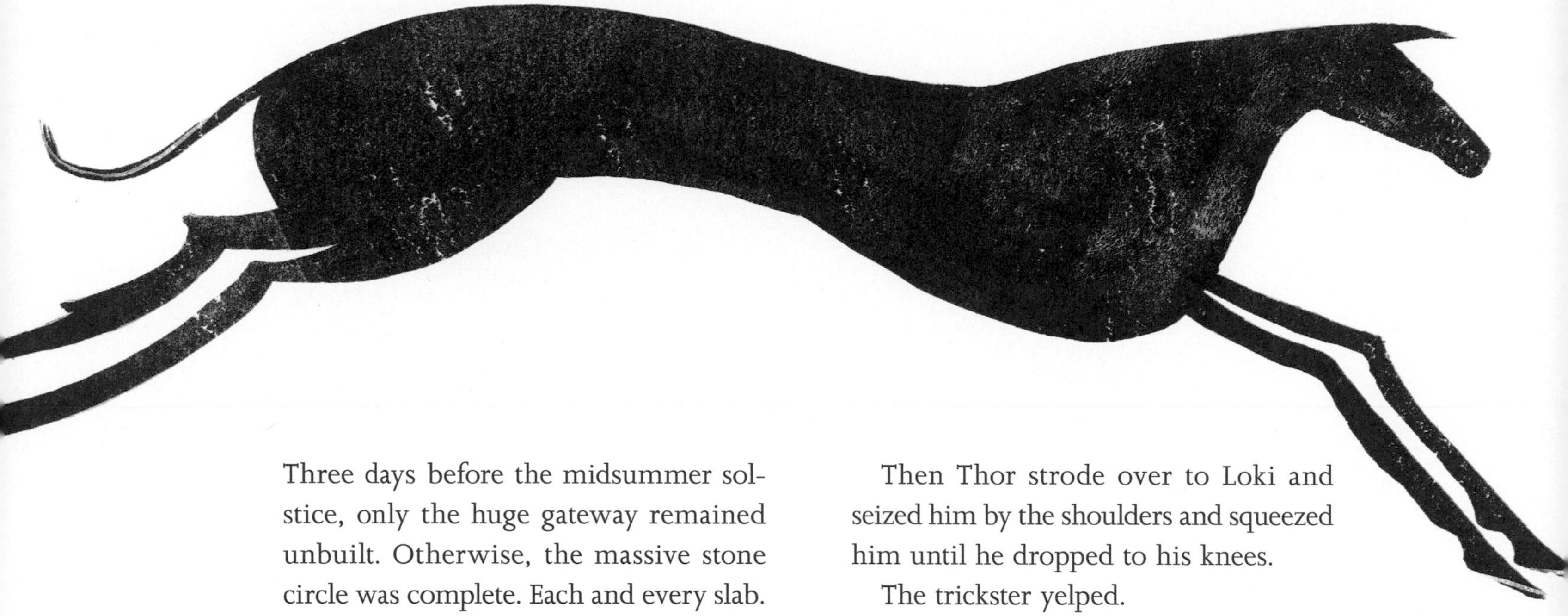

Three days before the midsummer solstice, only the huge gateway remained unbuilt. Otherwise, the massive stone circle was complete. Each and every slab.

Odin summoned all the gods and goddesses to his hall, and they stood in a circle around him.

"Our Freyja!" he called out. "Our Freyja will be sacrificed to a beast! Our world cast into darkness." Allfather wrapped his arms around himself and

Then Thor strode over to Loki and seized him by the shoulders and squeezed him until he dropped to his knees.

The trickster yelped.

"You got us into this, and you'll get us out of it." He squeezed again, and Loki howled. Like the tips of flames, his fox-eyes flickered with an idea.

■ ■ ■

The next night, the master-builder droned a grim sort of tune as he led Svadilfari down the well-worn track to the quarry, and in an ash-copse the birds listened, astonished that anything alive could make such an ugly sound.

And something else was listening.

A young mare.

She pricked up her elegant ears, and when Svadilfari and his master came close, she kicked up her golden shoes and hightailed it out of the copse.

The stallion heard her; he saw her; he smelt her; he wheeled round towards the

pranced in and out and round about. All night the stallion pursued her. And all night the mason chased them both, grunting and stumbling and tripping and cursing.

Driving her chariot made of sparks from Muspell, the Sun at last rose in the east.

The mason hammered the ground with his pickaxe. He knew that by losing a whole night's work, he would also lose his wager.

young mare, rose on his back legs, and snapped his reins.

The mare whisked her silver tail. She whinnied oh so seductively and, as the stallion galloped towards her, she turned back into the copse.

"No!" the mason bellowed. "No! No! Svadilfari!"

Far above, within their new walls, the gods and goddesses could hear him.

All night long the lusty young mare

"Tricked!" he yelled. "Tricked by good-for-nothings." He flailed at the trees all around him and brought them screeching and staggering to their knees.

The gods and goddesses hurried through the unbuilt gateway and down the track to the copse.

"Tricked by a gang of gods! A brothel of goddesses!"

The gods and goddesses could see how their mason was changing shape.

Expanding. Rising. As tall as the ash trees still left standing. He was a scowling rock-giant.

None of the gods dared go anywhere near him except for Thor. The god of thunder circled him, clockwise, anti-clockwise… He roared and with his right fist he smashed the giant's skull.

That same day, the gods and goddesses set to work on rebuilding the great gateway and, after that, their own high halls. They shouted and sang, and in time their fear, and then even the memory of their fear, began to fade.

"Save me from such memories," Freyja told Odin.

"Save me from losing them," Odin replied. "Who are we without memory?"

Only one thing, like a floodgate, stood in the way of the rising tide of the gods' peace of mind.

Loki's absence.

No one had seen him since the meeting in Gladsheim when Thor squeezed and threatened him, and no one had any idea where he had gone.

But one afternoon, five months later, the watchman Heimdall spotted him. The trickster was ambling up to the far end of Bifrost with a very young grey colt, and he appeared to be in no hurry to cross over.

Heimdall stared and rubbed his eyes. The colt had eight legs.

"Yes," said Loki. "Rather unusual, isn't he?" And then the shape-shifter whinnied just like the mare who had seduced the giant mason's stallion.

"Oh!" exclaimed Heimdall. "You didn't! Not a mare! Not even you…"

Loki just raised his orange eyebrows and laughed in Heimdall's face.

"What's his name?" asked Heimdall.

"Sleipnir. When he's full-grown, he'll be the fastest horse in the nine worlds."

Odin was glad to see Loki back. Not only did he actually rather like him, but when the trickster was back in Asgard, he could keep an eye on him. He was also greatly taken with the grey colt, who was still quite shaky on his legs.

"Where did you get him?" Allfather asked.

The shape-changer smiled such a strange smile, faint, then fierce and almost wild. "Ahh!" he murmured, as if he were remembering a long, long journey.

"Loki?"

"He's yours," said the trickster. "Take him, Odin. He'll carry you wherever you want: over land, across water, through thin air."

"Where did you get him?" Allfather asked again.

Loki narrowed his eyes. "Bone to bone," he said, "blood to blood. That's where I got him. As if we were glued together."

WHO  WE ARE

Everyone is someone in their own home.

Warriors and farmers and slaves, mused Odin. Some are wise, some are fools. Some are generous, some stingy. Some rely on themselves, some on others. Some are rich, some poor. Some beautiful, some ugly. Some are curious, and some blind to all the wonders of Midgard. And to tell the truth, ever since I and my brothers Vili and Ve fashioned the first human beings from two fallen trees — an ash and an elm — most people are a mix of all these things. Each person is made of many ingredients.

Odin reached up and stroked his raven Huginn, who was sitting on his right shoulder.

But one thing is missing, one thing from each man and woman and child on Middle Earth. Not one of them has a divine spark. Not one is a descendant of the gods.

For some while, Odin sat in his high seat, gazing out across the nine worlds.

I will send Heimdall, the son of nine mothers, to Middle Earth so that human beings will become more than flesh and blood and bone.

▪ ▪ ▪

How beautiful Middle Earth is. How sheerly beautiful, thought Heimdall, the watchman of the gods. *All the little ponds and pools noticing the sky. The rocks almost orange and bronze and seal-grey, the moss almost luminous.*

And how good to be alone...

All day the Sun hurried west, chased by the wolf Skoll, and just before dusk, the grey clouds closed around her.

Then white veils of rain drifted in, and Heimdall got soaked. He wasn't sorry when he saw a wooden hut with smoke rising from its turf roof. He knocked on the door, and the door creaked and swung open.

Heimdall ducked under the lintel and stepped into a smoky room. Sharp-eyed as he was, he could scarcely see the tip of his own nose.

Heimdall coughed. "Anyone at home?"

A very old man and woman, sitting on wooden tubs on either side of the fire, stretched and slowly stood up.

"Am I welcome?" asked Heimdall.

"All our guests are welcome," replied the old man.

"Not too welcome, I hope, or they'll eat you out of house and home."

The old woman cackled. "Without much trouble," she added.

When Heimdall's eyes were accustomed to the smoke and the half-light, the god could see how dingy and sparsely furnished the hut was. And yet it was all very neat and clean.

The marl floor was swept and glossy; the low pine table was scrubbed; and

the large, woollen rug was scruffy but unstained.

"We make do," the old woman observed. "This rain, though, it makes a right mess of our yard. All sludge and slime."

"Yes," Heimdall said. "Well, we must all make do. Humans aren't born equal. Each of us must make the most of ourselves."

"What is your name?" the old man asked politely.

"Rig," said Heimdall. "And yours, if I may ask."

"Edda," the old woman said. "Edda and Ai. Great-grandmother. Great-grandfather."

In the welcoming warmth of the hut, the drenched god began to steam like Edda's old iron pot, hanging over the fire.

The god sniffed. "I could eat a roasted ox," he declared.

"Not within these walls," said Edda

with a rueful smile. "But you're welcome to share what we have." And before long she gave the god a bowl of vegetable broth and hunks of husky bread.

They were sufficient to fill the god's stomach, though, and what with walking all day, he soon began to yawn.

"You can sleep between us," Edda told him. "That way, you won't feel the draught."

So that night the god lay in the middle of the rough reed matting in one corner of the room, and Edda spread the large woollen rug over all three of them. Indeed, Heimdall stayed for three nights, and then he thanked Ai and Edda for their warm welcome and went on his way.

Nine months passed, and Edda gave birth to a son.

He had thick black hair and from the moment he drew his first breath he certainly knew how to yell. Edda and Ai sprinkled fresh water over him and they called him Thrall.

From day to day and year to year Thrall looked more coarse – his skin was as rough as sandpaper, his knuckles were knotted, his spine was curved and his heels too big for his feet.

Still, no one could say he wasn't a good worker, ploughing, slopping out, spreading muck, feeding the hens, searching for deadwood in the forest, hauling awkward branches back home, chopping and stacking...

One day, though, Thrall found something else in the forest, something he couldn't take his eyes off. Her name was Thir. She was bandy-legged and her soles were damp and bark-stained; her arms were peeling and she had a squashed nose.

Thir liked the look of Thrall too, and before long they had a child, Fjosnir, the cowherd, and then twenty more!

Between them, they spread dung on the ploughed land around the hut, and built fences around the pigsty, and raised goats, and laid new green turf on the roof.

So Heimdall and Edda, and Thrall and Thir, and all their children, they are the ancestors of all the human beings living in Midgard who are poor and hungry and have to work for other people. And the divine spark shone within each one of them.

After Heimdall had left the hut belonging to great-grandmother and great-grandfather, he swung his arms, he stretched his legs, and walked for three days until he came to a well-kept farmhouse, although the barn right next to it wasn't in such good shape. It looked as if the corpse-eating eagle Hraesvelg had perched on the roof and given one flap of his wings and knocked the barn off balance.

A man raised the stout bar across the door of the farmhouse and Heimdall stepped in.

"Am I welcome?" asked the god.

"Everyone is welcome except for thieves and murderers," the farmer replied.

"Then I'm welcome!" said Heimdall with a smile. "And what a pleasing sight. To see you shaping up a new beam for the loom, and your wife weaving. You both look so smart – your combed hair and trimmed beard and leather jacket and breeches; your wife with her headband and smock and bronze shoulder brooches. I don't know! You make me look like a ragamuffin."

The farmer laughed. "Travellers are travellers. They all look the same. Yes, and I know that saying: 'As often as not, a man who sticks at home knows next to nothing about his guest.'"

The god smiled. "True enough!" he agreed.

"What is your name?" the farmer asked.

"Rig," said Heimdall. "And yours, may I ask?"

"Afi," the farmer replied. "Afi and Amma. Grandfather and grandmother."

Before very long, Amma laid on the table rye bread, and butter golden as a crocus, and a wooden platter heaped with boiled veal. Then she gave her guest a horn brimming with ale, and with one draught Heimdall drained it.

"Nothing better!" he announced. "Well, nothing except the horn that people can hear throughout the nine worlds."

"Oh," said Afi. "The ringing horn, you mean. The god Heimdall's horn."

"That's the one," said Heimdall, and he yawned. "What with walking all day, I'm ready for sleep."

At once grandfather and grandmother courteously offered their guest the best place, in the middle of the bed. And nine months later, Amma gave birth to a baby son.

Karl, that's what the farmer and his wife called him. He had chubby cheeks and sharp eyes.

While he was still a boy, Karl learned to drive oxen and fasten the share and coulter to a plough, as well as how to build a timber frame for a farmhouse or a barn, and how to pitch the roof.

Afi and Amma chose a wife for Karl – she was called Snör and very becoming she was. On her wedding day, she rode in a wagon to her new home, dressed in goatskin and wearing a veil, and she had a bunch of jangling keys secured at her waistband.

Before long Snör gave birth to a baby son. She and Karl called him Hal; and then they had eleven more sons and ten more daughters: Strong and Freeman and Craftsman, Beardy and Broad Shoulders, Slender and Proud and Bashful and Worthy and Graceful, all these and lots more.

They were happy.

So Heimdall and Amma, and Karl and Snör, and all their children, they are the ancestors of all the human beings living in Midgard who are freemen farmers. And the divine spark shone within each one of them.

After Heimdall had left the farmhouse belonging to grandmother and grandfather, he continued his journey and walked for three days. Then, in the blue hour, he came to a splendid building on a knoll overlooking the sea. The doors were wide open, and the passage inside was strewn with fresh rushes, laced with rosemary.

Sitting in the room at the heart of the house were Mothir and Fathir.

Fathir was twisting bowstrings and Mothir was watching him – well, watching him and smoothing her shift, and then inspecting her arms for blemishes, and arranging and re-arranging her forget-me-not gown. She was wearing two beautiful silver brooches between her shoulders and breasts. As for her neck! Ah, it was whiter than new snow.

"Am I welcome?" asked the god.

"But of course," replied Fathir. "Your name?"

"Rig," the god told him.

Mothir smiled. "Welcome, Rig,"

Mothir covered the table with a linen cloth and laid on it great delicacies: slices of white bread; silver dishes charged with well-browned horsemeat and grouse and partridge; red wine in a pitcher; silver wine-cups.

Rig and Fathir and Mothir ate and drank and talked until late, and then Rig slept between them on a mattress stuffed with the down of eider-duck.

Nine months later Mothir gave birth to Jarl – his hair was very fair, his cheeks were pink, and his eyes fearsome as those of an adder. And the divine spark shone within him.

Jarl learned how to thrust with a lance and parry with a shield; like Fathir, he learned how to twist a bowstring and how to loose arrows; he learned to ride and swim, and when was the right moment to unleash hounds hunting a fox or a wild boar.

One morning, when Jarl was older than a young boy and younger than a man, he saw someone striding out of the forest and straight towards him.

"Who are you?" asked Jarl.

"My name is Rig," said the man. He was carrying a bundle of red wooden markers, and each had several signs carved on it.

"What are they?" Jarl asked.

"Runes," the man told him. "Magic sounds. Secret meanings."

Jarl took one of the markers and examined the sign on it. "What's this one?" he asked.

"The sounds that put the wild sea to sleep."

Jarl looked up at Rig, and the god saw at once how excited he was.

"And this?"

"The song that blunts the blade of a sword."

"Really?"

Then Jarl and the god sat down in the long grass, and all morning Rig showed him the red markers, each painted with different signs, and taught him the runes of life, their sounds, their magic.

"And now I've this to tell you," the god said.

"What?" asked the boy. He looked flushed. He felt short of breath.

"Jarl, you are my son."

Jarl stared at Rig.

"I am Rig the King, and you will be Rig the King."

"But…"

Then Rig told Jarl how he had come to the hall, thirteen years before, and how he had met Mothir and Fathir. He embraced Jarl.

"Now is the time to leave home," he advised Jarl. "The time to win your land and a hall for yourself, the time to gather your own followers. Now is the time to win your name!"

That's what the young man did. He left home. He ranged far and wide. He gathered round him his own followers and won their loyalty with his leadership and gifts of gold armbands and rings. When warriors accused him of trampling over their land, and stealing their cattle and crops, he fought them. Jarl and his men stained the fields crimson.

By the time he was fully grown, Jarl owned no fewer than eighteen high halls, and his followers called him Rig the King.

Then Jarl sent messengers to a lord called Hersir, asking him for the hand of his daughter, Eina.

"What with her fine fingers and wrists and ankles, and her waterfall of fair hair," Hersir replied, "she may look delicate, but Jarl is making a shrewd choice. My daughter Eina! I've never met a young woman as accomplished and capable."

So Eina married Jarl, and she gave birth to twelve sons, and almost as many daughters. And the divine spark shone within each one of them.

Eina and Jarl's youngest son was called Kon; and when he was twelve, his father taught him the eighteen magic runes that Odin first learned when he hung for nine nights on Yggdrasill. Kon at once fell under their spell. For hour after hour, while his elder brothers were out in the field, hunting and learning their fighting skills, he sat and memorized the secret sounds, and learned how to sing-and-say them and cut-and-colour the markers for himself.

Kon learned how to cure sickness, and how to lighten a heavy, aching heart. He learned how to brace his arms and legs and snap ropes that bound him. He learned how to stop a flying arrow, and to blunt the blade of an enemy's sword; he learned how to quench flames and save a ship in a storm and win the love of a white-armed young woman; he learned how to loose a hanged man swinging from a gallows-tree and bring him back to life.

50

Yes, Kon learned the runes of life. And he knew that the magic you and you alone know is the strongest magic of all.

One afternoon Kon was ambling through the forest, amusing himself by calling down the birds and listening to them chatter.

A crow clapped down and perched on a branch right over his head. "Kon," it croaked. "What do you think you are doing?"

"Listening to you," said Kon. "That's what I'm doing. How do you know my name?"

"That's my business," said the crow, "but no one else will know it or listen to you unless you stop wasting your time seducing birds. Isn't it time you left home? Do you know how many young men are already winning followers, winning land and high halls, winning fame?"

Kon clenched his fists.

"Why have you learned the runes if not to put them to work? You must prove yourself! Claim the name of Young Kon the King!"

Kon's blood quickened. It began to whirl round his body. "I will answer you," he called up to the crow. "I'll answer you with my shining sword. Yes, I'll sign it with the blood of my enemies."

So the children of Heimdall and Mothir, and Jarl and Eina, they are the ancestors of all the human beings living in Midgard who are nobly born. The divine spark shone within each one of them.

It was Odin who raised the elm tree and the ash tree, and breathed the spirit of life into them. But because of Heimdall, each woman and man and child on Middle Earth is descended from the gods.

MOUTHFULS OF POETRY

Music and poetry

master the world.

Thor and Loki walked together across the Plain of Ida towards Odin's hall Valaskjalf. And Loki amused himself by seeing how long he could kick the same stone along the path, but he kept darting in front of Thor and getting in his way until the god of thunder kicked the stone himself. He kicked it right over the wall of Asgard.

"Why has Odin summoned us?" Thor grumbled. "What does he want?"

"How should I know?" Loki said. "You're his son."

"Most of us are!" said Thor. "But that doesn't mean we know what he's thinking."

Odin was waiting inside his hall, and he asked each of the gods and goddesses to spit into a large spittoon, made of seven metals. Not Loki though — to be sure, the trickster lived in Asgard but he was the son of a giant and a giantess.

"Now that we've all mixed our saliva," Odin announced, "the old enmity between the Warrior Gods and the Green-and-Gold Gods will be nothing but memory. Distant thunder."

Allfather scooped a large glob of spittle out of the spittoon. Between his hands it shone and trembled like frogspawn.

"With this," he told everyone, "I will shape a new kind of being."

This supernatural being, half god and half man, the gods called Kvasir. And because of the way he was created, he knew everything there is to know. The gods loved him dearly, and Kvasir was always generous with his wisdom, and often ranged through Midgard, counselling men and women and helping children to answer their own questions.

When the dwarf brothers Fjalar and Galar got to hear about Kvasir, they could think of little else but his precious hoard of wisdom, and how, as they thought, he was just squandering it. They wanted to steal it for themselves, and before long they invited Kvasir to a feast in their cliff-cave beside the shore — the shore of the great ocean that surrounds Midgard.

When he arrived, wise Kvasir found more than one hundred dwarfs had gathered to welcome him, some with greedy little eyes gleaming like green glow-worms, some with twisted bodies and some with twisted minds.

Kvasir smiled and shook his head. "Nothing I say will match the honour you do me."

There were flickering candles on the stone tables and tucked into cracks in the walls, and the rock floor was strewn with little glittering quartz crystals. No warm wall-hangings, nothing but jaundiced stalagmites and dripping stalactites.

Kvasir admired the tableware. Every dish and platter and knife and spoon was made of hammered gold.

"How wise you are not to stow away all your gold but to put it to work and use it," Kvasir said.

After the feast, Fjalar and Galar offered to show Kvasir their secret chamber. He followed them out of the echoing feasting-hall, and as soon as the three of them were on their own, the dwarfs drew pointed knives from their sleeves. They drove them deep into wise Kvasir's heart.

For a little while Kvasir's heart went on pumping and his blood spurted out of it; then it streamed, then it dribbled, and the two brothers caught it all — every single drop — in two large metal jars and a gold cauldron they called Heart Stirrer.

That same night, as soon as all their guests had trooped off to their own gloomy caves and fissures and potholes, Fjalar and Galar added liquid honey to the three containers and, with long-handled gold ladles, mixed it with the congealing blood.

This blend of blood and honey formed the most sublime mead.

"Heavenly!" Fjalar said.

"Holy!" said Galar. "Whoever drinks a measure of this mead will become a wise poet."

"And there's nothing in the nine worlds better than that," his brother added.

Before long Odin sent messengers to Fjalar and Galar to enquire when Kvasir would be returning to Asgard, and at once the two dwarfs replied that Kvasir had most unfortunately choked on a large lump of his own knowledge, and that since there was no one who knew as much as he did, no one had been able to help him.

■ ■ ■

From time to time some dwarfs and giants feasted together. Although dwarfs hiss and whisper and giants boast and bawl, they usually enjoyed one another's company. But when the giant Gilling and his wife visited Fjalar and Galar, it didn't work out so well.

Gilling drank so much that he almost lost his wits, and despite his wife's efforts to shut him up, he argued with absolutely everything the two dwarfs said. As the evening wore on, he became more and more embittered and spiteful.

Eventually Fjalar said, "What a nasty piece of work you are!" and at once

Gilling stood up and threw the feasting table onto its back.

"Nasty!" bellowed the giant. "Is that what you said?"

Gilling's wife slapped her right hand over her husband's mouth, and Fjalar looked at Galar.

"A dose of sea air, perhaps," Fjalar suggested. "Why don't we take your husband out for a row? That'll help bring him to his senses."

So the two dwarfs went rowing with Gilling. They rowed out into deep water and rammed their boat into a slimy, dripping rock.

Gilling shouted with alarm, and when he tried to stand up, he stumbled against a gunwale and capsized the boat.

The giant was unable to swim, so that was the end of him.

The dwarfs righted their boat, but it was still awash with slopping sea-water, so they rowed rather slowly back to land.

"Such an awful accident," Galar told Gilling's wife, and he pulled a long face.

Fjalar shook his head. "If only he had been able to swim."

Gilling's wife gulped. She couldn't stop weeping and sobbing, and before long the two dwarfs could feel the tide of her tepid tears washing around their ankles, and they didn't like it.

Then Fjalar whispered something, and his brother scampered out of the feasting-hall and down a narrow passage.

"Let's put our noses outside," Fjalar told Gilling's wife. "I can point out the rock to you. The place where your poor husband…"

So the dwarf led Gilling's wife across the hall and politely stood aside so that

she could walk through the low, narrow passage.

"Mind your head," he warned her.

Galar was ready and waiting. And the moment the giantess stepped out of the passage, he dropped a millstone onto her head. It crushed her skull.

"I was sick and tired of all her bawling," said Fjalar.

"She was just a lump of blubber," Galar agreed. "Frankly, we've done all the other giants a favour."

But the giant Suttung, the son of Gilling and his wife, did not see things in this way.

When word of his father's and mother's deaths reached him, he hurried out of Jotunheim and headed for Fjalar and Galar's cave.

Suttung listened impatiently to their tall tale, and then he grabbed them. Holding one squirming dwarf in each hand, he stumped out of the cave and across the foreshore, and waded a long way out to sea.

"You dwarfs may be able to swim," he growled, "but not this far. Not from here right back to land."

He dropped them onto a flat rock just above the jumping waves. "So when the tide rises…" Suttung said.

Fjalar and Galar glumly eyed each other. Then they nodded.

"We've an idea," said Fjalar.

"Give us our lives, and we'll give you our greatest treasure," his brother said.

"What treasure?" growled Suttung.

Standing in the water up to his waist, the giant listened to how Kvasir had been created by the gods and how the dwarfs had mixed his blood with honey. As Galar went on, Suttung began to roll his saucer eyes. Once he owned it … he could make up songs for galumphing

… he could do anything … he could make up poems in praise of himself… Why! He could become King of the Giants. What's more, Suttung knew how infuriated and anxious the gods and goddesses would be when they heard that he had got the mead.

So the giant agreed to exchange the lives of the two miserable dwarfs for the mead, and he carried the two jars and the gold cauldron containing them straight back to Hnitbjorg, the mountain where he lived with his daughter Gunnlod.

Suttung hacked out a room in the very middle of the mountain. That's where he hid the mead. Then he told his daughter Gunnlod that she had one duty and one only.

"Gunnlod, guard this mead, this gift of poetry and wisdom without which life is scarcely worth living – that's what the gods say. Guard it by day and guard it by night."

Because giants are boastful, and can't keep secrets, it wasn't long before the gods and goddesses heard about the divine mead and how Suttung had come by it, and where he had hidden it.

"I'll go to Hnitbjorg," Thor offered at once. "I'm not having Suttung get the better of us."

"In that case, I'll come with you," Loki said. "Brawn is not much use without brains. Anyhow, everyone knows how thirsty you get. You'd probably drink half the mead on the way back to Asgard."

"No," declared Allfather. "I'll go to Jotunheim myself, and do whatever I must to get the mead back. Kvasir was made of each of us and all of us, and his blood belongs to us. The gift of poetry is only ours to give."

Wearing a thick woollen cloak and a broad-brimmed hat to conceal his blind eye, Odin left Asgard on foot. He greeted Heimdall, crossed the three-strand rainbow and set off for the broad river away to the north that divides Midgard from Jotunheim. A ferryman rowed him across and Odin strode up into swelling foothills. Well-watered as they were with summer showers, the grassy valleys between them were

58

green and shining and succulent, and strewn with wildflowers – ox-eye daisies and willowherb, scabious and burning gentian.

Allfather walked down towards a line of nine young men scything in a large field. They were dripping with sweat.

"Hard work, lads?" Odin called out.

One youth leaned on his long scythe. "Want a go, do you?"

"Are you from Midgard?" Allfather asked.

The youth nodded. "Hired hands. We're here all summer. I'm the foreman."

"Who are you working for?"

"Baugi. You know, Suttung's brother."

"Ah!" exclaimed Odin.

"All autumn too," groaned another lad. "With blunt scythes."

"Sharpen them," Odin said.

"Can't."

"Why not?"

The lad scratched his right ear. "Er … why can't we, mate?" he asked the foreman. "Why did you say?"

"Because we got no whetstone."

"That's right," said the lad. He shook his head. "We ain't got no whetstone," he explained to Odin.

Allfather untied the top of his long coat, and pulled out a whetstone. It looked like a rolling-pin with tapering ends.

"Use mine," he told the foreman. "No! Give me your scythes, the whole lot of you, and I'll put edges on them. You lads need a break."

The nine scythes were soon so sharp they could have cut thistles and thorns. They could have cut the lads' fingernails and toenails.

"How could we, well…" their foreman began. "Seeing as we don't get paid until we've done all this work – can you loan us it? That whetstone."

Allfather stared at him and his one eye glittered, black and silver. Then he glared at each of the other lads, and his gaze was so fearsome it drilled right through them. Odin whirled his arm and hurled the whetstone as high as the bubbling larks.

"Catch it, lads!" he shouted, and his voice was as cruel as the cutting-edges

of their scythes. "My whetstone belongs to whoever catches it."

The hired hands stared up into the bald, bright sky. They brandished their scythes, they yelled and spun round, they swept and spun round again like dancers in a trance. Like lost boys.

By the time the whetstone had fallen back to earth, all the lads had accidentally cut one another's throats competing for the whetstone; all nine lay higgledy-piggledy in the blood-stained grass. As for Odin, he caught the whetstone, replaced it inside his cloak and springheeled further into the foothills leading up to towering blue mountains.

Hundreds, maybe thousands, of sheep and goats were scattered across the high pastures and, although he couldn't see anyone, Odin several times heard the shrill call of some herdsman.

Allfather walked on. But when he came to the very foot of a rocky mountain, he doubled right back on his tracks, hurried across the slopes, and, after a couple of hours, strode up to the giant Baugi's farm. The size of the hay-barn astonished him. You could have stowed four or five barns built by human beings inside it, or even a couple of the halls of the great gods.

"Who are you?" Baugi demanded.

"Bolverk," said Allfather. "Have you got any summer work for me?"

Baugi kept clenching and unclenching his fists, and looking over the god's shoulder at the open door. "Bad!" he growled through his broken teeth.

"What's bad?" asked Odin.

"Terrible!"

"What is?"

"All my young farmhands have been murdered."

"No!"

"This afternoon!" snarled the giant. "All nine of them. It must have been raiders! I'll run them down and kill them!"

"Good timing!" Odin said. "Good timing, then."

"Good?"

"I've come just at the right moment," Odin told him. "I can do the work of nine men. And I'll stay all summer."

The giant gave Odin a suspicious look. "Is that so?" he growled. "What did you say your name is?"

"Bolverk."

"And your price?"

Odin shrugged. "Oh," he said quite casually, "to be strong as nine, let alone as strong as a giant, that's a great thing. Very great. But to be a poet, I think that's the greatest. My price? Just one sip of Suttung's mead."

The giant hawked and spat on the ground. "I'm not my brother's keeper," he said. "Suttung would never agree to it. He never agrees to anything."

"That's a pity," said Odin, and he sucked his cheeks.

"Work well for me all summer and I'll ask him," Baugi told him. "That's the best I can do."

So Odin laboured in the giant's fields all that summer. He cut the grass and trussed it and hauled it back to the huge barn; he watered Baugi's cattle and sheared his sheep.

"Now then!" he reminded Baugi at the end of the summer season. "You're going to keep your word."

"You're not a mere man," the giant grumbled. "I don't know who you are, but I know that."

Odin smiled a smile as sharp as a scythe. "You keep your word," he said, "and you'll come to no harm."

So Baugi visited his brother at Hnitbjorg, where his daughter Gunnlod was guarding the divine mead.

"Over my dead body," Suttung told him. "No one is going to taste so much as a drop of it."

When Baugi returned to his farm and told Odin what his brother had said, Odin was angry. "All right," he said. "If your brother won't give me a single gulp, we'll have to steal it." He delved into the inner pocket of his cloak and with a flourish produced a wicked-looking screw used for boring holes in wood and metal and stone.

"This is an auger," he said, "and it's not an ordinary one. It can drill through ice, drill through hardwood and through granite. The least you can do for me is drill a hole through the mountain where Gunnlod is guarding the mead. Anyhow, don't you fancy a drop yourself?"

Baugi did as Odin asked him. With the auger he drilled into Hnitbjorg. Then he pulled it out and wiped his brow. "There!" he exclaimed. "That's it."

Odin put his mouth to the hole made by the auger. He filled his lungs and blew hard and a shower of rock chippings blew straight back into his face.

The god glared at Baugi. "That's not right through!" he shouted. "It's not, and you know it."

Angrily, Baugi drilled again, vowing to get his own back on Odin, and when Odin blew into the hole for the second time, all the rock chippings rough-and-tumbled right through the mountain and out the other side.

At once Odin turned himself into a snake and, before Baugi could stab him with the point of the auger, he slid into the passage and writhed towards the chamber at the heart of the mountain. Then Odin changed himself back into Bolverk – tall and strong-shouldered and muscular: a man of a god, a godlike man.

Gunnlod, Suttung's daughter, was guarding the mead. As soon as she saw Bolverk, she was as spellbound by her one-eyed visitor as he seemed to be spellbound by her. On her gold stool she sat and listened to his stories and songs of the nine worlds. She listened to stories of times long past and times present, and it was as if, in that chamber, time no longer existed. After being imprisoned in the cold chamber and in deafening silence for so long, Gunnlod felt that these stories were warming her back to life.

The giant's daughter swept back her long, ashen hair and Bolverk gazed into her trusting eyes. He took her in his arms; he kissed her and kissed her. And they lay together for three nights.

Gunnlod was so drunk with passion that she completely forgot, or chose to forget, her father's words. When Bolverk asked her for three gulps of the divine mead, she actually took his hand and led him to the two jars and the cauldron.

With his first gulp Bolverk emptied all the mead in the first jar and with the next all the mead in the second. He held both draughts in his mouth. And then, with his third huge gulp, he emptied Heart Stirrer, the gold cauldron, and held that in his mouth too. At once he turned himself into an eagle and, leaving Gunnlod behind without a backward glance, he flapped away down the dark passage.

Suttung was sitting outside his hall at the foot of the mountain and, because he had won the gift of wisdom by sampling the divine mead himself, he knew what must have happened as soon as he saw the eagle soaring towards Asgard.

The giant crouched and chanted the magic sounds known only to those who have tasted the mead, and he too was able to

change himself into an eagle. At once he set off in pursuit of Odin.

The watchman Heimdall was first to see them – two eagles, one chasing the other and screaming. At once he sounded his ringing horn, and the goddesses and gods brought out pans and bowls and cauldrons from their halls, and laid them on the ground just inside the great wall.

The nearer the two eagles came, the closer Suttung drew to Odin because the god was weighed down by all the mead in his mouth. Several times, Suttung tried to peck at Odin's tailfeathers, and when the god flew over the bridge and dived over the gods' newly built wall, there was no more than a heartbeat between them. Such was Odin's haste that he accidentally spilled a few drops of mead outside the wall and they fell onto the ground. The gods and goddesses weren't worried about them, though, and later Odin said that any human who found a drop was welcome to it. He said it was the right amount for anyone and everyone who wants to make up a cheery jingle or a rhyme.

When Odin spat the divine mead into the crocks and containers, all the gods and goddesses recognized just how important their new wall was. Allfather sucked his cheeks and spat again, and Suttung soared above the watching gods, wild and shrieking. He knew that if he tried to land inside Asgard, the gods would overwhelm him and tear him to pieces. He screamed, he wheeled away and dropped towards Jotunheim.

The gods used cunning and force, and knew they could never trust the giants and the dwarfs not to do the same. And sometimes men and women use cunning and force. So does trust belong only to children and young men and women – young as the hired hands from Midgard who accidentally cut each other's throats competing for Odin's whetstone? Is there no one else in the nine worlds so full of shining trust that it will never be eclipsed by the cunning and force around them?

One by one, the gods and goddesses tasted the mead made of wise Kvasir's blood and molten honey. And because the god Bragi so loved words for their music and meaning, and was never at a loss for them, Odin named him the god of poetry.

Allfather allowed Bragi a double portion of mead. He charged him with remembering all the stories about the gods and goddesses, and sometimes singing-and-saying them at their feasts.

Time passed, as time must, and just now and then Allfather crossed the rainbow bridge and offered a sip of the divine mead to someone in Midgard. And each man or woman who tasted it became a poet.

THREE GRISLY CHILDREN

A young wolf and a croaking raven: no one should be such a fool as to trust them.

There was peace in Asgard. The gods and goddesses felt safe within their newly built walls, and even though they mourned the loss of Kvasir, Allfather had retrieved the precious mead made from his blood and honey.

"But we haven't seen Loki for rather a long time," said Allfather, "and neither has his wife Sigyn. I wonder where he is, and what he's up to."

One day, Honir, the god whose legs were so long that all the other gods except Thor had to run to keep up with him, came back to Midgard with alarming news.

"Three children!" exclaimed Odin. "You're telling me that Loki has fathered three children?"

"And their mother's not Sigyn but a giantess," Honir said. "Angrboda. That's what I've heard."

"Loki is quite dangerous enough as it is," said Odin. "We almost lost Freyja because of him."

"And the Sun and the Moon," added Honir.

"Three children," repeated Thor. "Let's do away with them."

"Not so fast," said Odin. "Let's have a look at them." And he instructed Thor and Honir to lead a group of gods to the lair of the giantess Angrboda, kidnap her three children and bring them back to Asgard without Loki knowing anything about it.

"They're his children," Allfather told them, "and he may love them, even if we do not. He may care for them."

When all the gods and goddesses saw Loki's three children, they were astonished and appalled.

The eldest child was a monster serpent called Jormungand. His eyes were like charcoal moons and his body was almost as thick as the trunk of the ash tree Yggdrasill itself.

As soon as Odin saw him, he knew that, fully grown, the serpent would be even more dangerous than a whole posse of giants.

"Take him away," Allfather commanded. "Take him to the place where he can do least harm."

But Jormungand kept growing larger and larger even as the gods stared at him, and it needed no fewer than

seven gods and their servants to carry the monster, threshing and thrashing, all the way to the ocean. They threw him in, and when he was fully grown, the serpent Jormungand was so long that he was able to wrap around the whole of Midgard and bite on his own tail.

Loki and Angrboda's second child was a daughter called Hel, and she was one half living woman and one half corpse; her eyes were sunken and her expression was grim.

Allfather took one look at Hel and dropped her right down into the darkness and freezing mist beneath the bottom root of Yggdrasill. The realm where she lived was called by her own name, Hel, and that's where she had her enormous hall and admitted everyone who had died of illness or old age.

Loki and Angrboda's third child looked less of a problem. He was a wolf cub called Fenrir and, even though he was rather large, the gods allowed him to roam around the Plain of Ida.

"We can keep an eye on him from day to day," Odin told the other gods.

Nevertheless, only one god was fearless enough to approach Fenrir and feed him with haunches of meat, and that was Odin's brave son, Tyr.

Fenrir grew so fast that the goddesses were alarmed and said he looked larger every time they saw him.

"Have you heard the sound he makes when he cracks bones?" Freyja asked.

"And the way he stares at us?" said the goddess Idun.

Several of the gods went down to the Well of Urd, which was under the topmost root of Yggdrasill, and asked the three Norns who lived there what they should do with the wolf cub.

"His mother is evil and his father is worse," the Norn called Fate told them.

"He'll fight against the gods in the last battle," the Norn called Being warned them.

The third Norn, Necessity, nodded gravely. "Worse," she said, "much worse. Fenrir will bring about their downfall."

In silence the gods listened, and in silence they left. They knew they couldn't stain holy Asgard with blood even though Fenrir was growing more dangerous day by day. They didn't know what to do.

"We are the gods," Allfather told them, "and Fenrir's nothing but a wolf cub. We know much more than he does, so we must use our knowledge to trick him. Sometimes cunning is the best way."

"I know what we can do," said Njord, the father of Freyr and Freyja. He had spent long enough in the shipyards in Midgard to know about bollards and grappling irons and moorings and

anchors, and was able to forge an iron chain called Laeding.

"Very good!" pronounced Odin, and he approached Fenrir with the chain. "You see this?" he asked. "You see how strong it is?"

Fenrir bared his teeth in a kind of smile, and inspected the chain. "It's not very well made," he said, "but I can see it's not weak."

"It's certainly stronger than you," Odin provoked him.

"Never!" snarled Fenrir.

Then the wolf cub allowed the gods to truss him with Laeding, so that he was scarcely able to move.

"Ready?" asked the wolf. And without waiting for an answer, he flexed his neck and tightened every muscle in his body, he groaned, and all at once the links of Laeding sprang apart, and Fenrir raced off across the Plain of Ida, howling.

"Make another chain," Odin instructed Njord. "Make it twice as thick, and this time be sure the links are really well forged. It needs to be larger than the largest anchor chain in Midgard."

This chain was called Dromi, and it took three of the gods to drag it up to Asgard.

"Your life here is worthless," Odin told Fenrir.

Fenrir swung his head from side to side.

"Exactly," said Odin. "Unless we win fame for our great deeds, our lives will be without meaning. But you, Fenrir, if you can prise apart this chain – if you can snap it – you'll be famed for your strength throughout the nine worlds."

Fenrir inspected Dromi and padded slowly round it. "Fame and risk, risk and fame," he growled. "They're yoked together."

And that was all he had to say as the gods heaved and strained and coiled the huge chain round and round Fenrir's massive neck and body and legs.

In front of the gods and goddesses, the wolf seemed to expand. He did expand!

He braced every single muscle in his body and the gods could hear Dromi grinding, grating and scarcely able to take the strain. Then Fenrir somehow rolled and waddled over to one of the large rocks in the plain and summoned up all his strength and slammed his body into it.

Dromi exploded. The gods dived for cover, and some of the iron links flew halfway to the stars.

In the safety of his own hall, Odin summoned the gods and goddesses. "Sometimes," he said, "not even cunning is sufficient. We must use magic as well."

He beckoned Freyr's messenger, shining Skirnir, whose body is so bright

70

it lights his way
through the dark.
Allfather asked him to
go down to the dwarfs and
to promise them that if they
could forge a chain to fetter Fenrir,
the gods would reward them with their
own weight in gold.

At once eight dwarfs got to work. In their
gloomy cave, their green eyes glowed, and they
made a long ribbon called Gleipnir, suave and soft.

As soon as he got back to Asgard, Skirnir pre-
sented the ribbon to Allfather.

Odin fingered it. He frowned. "Not silk," he said.

"Almost slithery. What's it made of?"

"Six things," Skirnir told him. "The sound a cat makes as it moves. The beard of a woman. A mountain's roots, and a bear's tendons. The breath of a fish. Yes, and a bird's saliva."

"How can that be?" exclaimed Thor.

"Even if it is," Odin said, "I very much doubt whether we'll be able to bind Fenrir with it."

Skirnir smiled. "Each dwarf is as horrible as the next," he said, "and they're extremely greedy, but they're not liars. And I can explain how they're not lying now."

"How?" demanded Thor.

"Have you ever wondered why a prowling cat makes no sound? Have you ever stopped to think why women don't grow beards? True, you can't dig up a mountain but there are many things that seem not to exist, but are actually treasured and used by the dwarfs."

So the gods walked back to the Plain of Ida, led by Tyr the brave god of war, and, keeping close for comfort, they slowly approached Fenrir.

"Would you like to see Lyngvi?" Freyja asked him.

"What?"

"Heather Island. There in the middle of the lake."

"Why?" asked the wolf.

"We're all going over there for a feast, and as you've never even been there…"

So Tyr and Heimdall rowed Fenrir across the lake in a barge – he stood in the prow and the gods and goddesses jammed themselves in the stern – and when they got to the little island, Odin pulled the dwarfs' ribbon, Gleipnir, out of his pocket. He dangled it in front of the wolf.

"Will you risk it?" he asked. "Will you let me tie you up?"

"Risk?" said Fenrir. "I'd be able to snap that with my teeth, and where's the fame in that?"

"This ribbon may be a little stronger than you think," Odin replied. "To tell you the truth, we don't know ourselves."

Fenrir growled. "Don't know?" he said. "You don't know? Well, if there's magic in it, you can keep it. I'm not having you weave magic around my legs."

"I thought you were strong," said Thor.

"I am."

"Stronger than iron chains."

"If you can't rip … rip this pretty

little ribbon," lovely Freyja said, "we'll set you free anyhow. You can trust us."

"Trust you?" snapped Fenrir. "I don't trust you. If ever you fetter me, it will be thousands of years before you release me." The wolf loped round and round the group of gods. "I don't want to be bound," he said, "but I don't want it said that I'm a coward either." Fenrir stopped right in front of Allfather. "All right! Bind me, but one of you must put his hand inside my mouth, so that I know you're not double-crossing me."

The gods and goddesses lowered their eyes. They said nothing. But then brave Tyr raised his right arm and placed his hand between Fenrir's jaws.

At once the gods wound the ribbon round Fenrir, and the more he strained and struggled and jerked, the tighter it grew.

The wolf snarled. His eyes blazed. Then he clamped his jaws, and Tyr shrieked.

All the gods and goddesses shouted, they waved their arms and laughed. They all laughed except Tyr: he lost his right hand.

The gods knotted the ribbon to a chain, and they threaded the chain through a huge rock with a hole in it, and looped it back on itself. Then they dug a deep hole and pushed the rock until it toppled into it, and they dropped another rock on top of that.

Fenrir grated and ground his teeth, but when he stretched his bloody jaws, Heimdall jammed his sword between them so that the wolf was unable to close his mouth.

Fenrir was fettered. He was gagged. All day and all night the wolf slavered – and a milky river of his spittle and saliva streamed from Heather Island into the lake.

So Jormungand, the monster serpent, waits at the bottom of the salt-sea surrounding Midgard, biting on his own tail. In the darkness and freezing mist, Hel sits in her hall of the dead. And on the little island of Lyngvi, in the middle of the lake, the wolf Fenrir waits.

And the gods and goddesses? They kept remembering the warnings of the Norns that the wolf Fenrir would fight in the last battle and bring about their downfall. They wondered about where in the nine worlds Loki had got to. And they were anxious about what the trickster would do when he came back to Asgard and found out the fate of his three grisly children.

"He'll want to take revenge," said Odin. "But whatever he does, it would be even worse for us if we had done nothing."

APPLES OF YOUTH

The treachery of a friend is worse than the treachery of an enemy.

When Loki at last returned to Asgard, he soon found out what had happened to his three children. He smouldered; he shook with rage. And he planned to take revenge as soon as he could.

And yet the trickster was fascinated by the gods – their power and their knowledge. He enjoyed their company, and liked nothing more than to go travelling with Thor, or with Odin and long-legged Honir…

It was June and almost midnight. The Sun drifted then dipped just under the horizon, and Midgard became very still. The land, the lakes and the mountains away to the north were lost in dreams of themselves.

But Odin, Loki and Honir had heard and smelt and seen quite enough for one day – a mountain belching and smoking, a stinking lake, a steaming rock pool where they all swam and a thundering waterfall. Much as they enjoyed discovering places they had never visited before, they were mind-weary and limb-weary, and interested only in their own stomachs, and the smell and taste of roast meat.

"We set out to explore," Loki complained, "not to endure."

"If only Heimdall were here," said Honir, "he'd be able to spy out food and shelter."

But then Loki saw an ox not at all far off, and while he chased and killed it, Odin and Honir collected sticks and lit a fire next to a great oak tree, the only one for miles around. They chopped the beast's shoulders and rump into four huge joints, and as soon as they smelt them roasting, their spirits rose.

For some reason, though, the meat was very slow to cook. Loki kept poking the fire with his staff, and turning the joints over, but they remained bloody and almost raw.

"Just a little longer," Odin said. "It never hurts to wait for what's worthwhile."

The fire crackled; the meat spat. Time passed.

"It must be ready now," Honir said. "Don't you think so? What do you think?"

"What I think," said Loki, "is that never once in my life have I heard you make up your own mind. Keep quiet, Honir!"

Then the trickster raked the branches and again turned the joints of meat over, but they were still uncooked.

"Something's stopping this meat from roasting," Odin said. "Some kind of magic is stopping us from eating it."

"Something up here!" croaked a voice in the oak tree.

The three gods looked up and saw an enormous eagle, perched on a branch above them.

"I'm as hungry as you are," the eagle croaked. "If you let me eat my fill, I'll let your meat roast."

At once the bird swooped down from the tree. He seized both the shoulder joints between his talons and both joints of the rump as well.

Then he flapped back to the foot of the oak and, crouching there, he tore at the meat and glared at the gods.

Loki was enraged. He jumped up, grabbed his staff with both hands and rammed it right into the bird's body.

The eagle screeched and dropped all the meat. He beat his huge wings and launched himself into the air, and Loki couldn't let go of the staff because of the eagle's magic. Both his hands were fastened to it, and the other end of the staff was still stuck in the bird's body.

The eagle didn't soar. No, he skimmed just a few feet above the ground for miles and miles so that the trickster's ankles, knees, shoulders and elbows were grazed by thorns and thistles, and scraped and bloodied by outcrops of rock.

"Help!" yelled Loki. "Help!"

The eagle took no notice.

"Help!" implored Loki. "You're not deaf!"

"Deaf to you," the eagle replied.

"You're pulling my arms out of my sockets. Help!"

"Only," croaked the bird, "if you agree to this. Bring Idun and her apples of youth over the rainbow bridge and out of Asgard."

"Who are you?" yelled Loki.

The eagle flopped onto the ground and glared at Loki.

"A rock-giant? A frost-giant?"

"Thiazi!" screeched the giant-eagle, and Loki covered his ears. "Thiazi! The frost-giant! Go on! Swear it! Get down on your knees."

"I swear it," said Loki. "I'll bring Idun and her apples out of Asgard. I'll find some way."

"I'll be waiting," Thiazi told him. Then the eagle shook himself free from the staff, released Loki's hands from the other end and soared away towards the high mountains in the realm of the giants, while Loki slowly made his way back to Odin and Honir, only to find that they had already eaten almost all the meat and left without him.

■ ■ ■

The trickster knew that the gods and goddesses depended on the goddess Idun's apples for their youth. And he knew how, without them, they would very quickly become anxious, and begin to grow old.

Painfully, he limped back to Asgard, and he was still working out what to do when he saw Idun standing in the great gateway.

"Ah!" he said. "I've been looking for you. You'll never believe this."

Idun always wanted to believe others. She was as rosy as an apple herself, and when she smiled everyone else found that they were smiling too.

"No, you won't believe it."

"Why not?" asked Idun.

"No one believes me," Loki told her,

79

slowly shaking his head, "even when I'm telling the truth."

"Tell me, Loki."

Loki felt uneasy. It was one thing to trick mighty Odin or the thunder god Thor – and since the gods had captured his three children, he was eager to do so – but quite another to deceive this young goddess, so trusting, and so easy to mislead.

"Well," said Loki, "you'll have to see this for yourself. Down in Midgard, I've found a tree thick with apples, and they're made of gold. I've never seen anything like them except the ones in your basket. We must pick them and bring them back to Asgard."

Idun stroked Loki's arm, and gently smiled. "What a strange creature you are," she said. "So … contrary. One moment so considerate, one moment so unkind."

"They're not far beyond the rainbow bridge," Loki told her. "Not far at all. Come with me and I'll show you."

Carrying her basket of golden apples over one arm, Idun followed Loki over Bifrost, and as soon as he saw her coming, Thiazi turned himself into an eagle again. The frost-giant swooped and lifted Idun and her basket of apples in his talons and carried her to his fortress high in the mountains, while Loki hid himself in a haystack.

Boom of avalanche; clatter of rockfall; wind-whistle, wind-scream. Looking out through one of the wind-eyes in the cold stone fortress, Idun covered the shells of her ears with her hands, and she trembled.

"This is your new home," roared the giant. "Here you are and here you'll stay. Without you and your apples, the gods will age, they'll soon grow old. But I, Thiazi, and my daughter, Skadi, we'll remain young for ever."

■ ◪ ■

Heimdall, watchman of the gods, had seen Loki leading Idun over the rainbow bridge and, sharp-eyed as he was, he could see an enormous eagle swooping on the goddess and lifting her and her apples away. Three times he blew his horn to summon all the gods and goddesses to their great meeting-place, the hall of Gladsheim.

"We must find Loki," Odin told them. "Wherever he is."

The gods searched their own halls. With their servants, the light elves, they scattered through the fields and combed the copses and woods, and Thor rowed Tyr out to the middle of the lake in case Loki had gone to visit his grisly son on Heather Island.

But all this time, Loki was asleep on

top of the haystack just the other side of Bifrost. Freyr found him and grabbed him by the scruff of his neck before he was fully awake.

Loki squirmed. He protested.

"You're coming with me," said Freyr, "and you can count on a warm welcome."

Once more, Heimdall sounded his ringing horn, and the weary gods trooped back to Gladsheim.

Odin was sitting in his high seat, and he stood up as soon as Loki walked in. "You again!" he shouted. "Where's Idun?"

"It's true," Loki admitted. "I tempted Idun over the rainbow bridge. But I had to. I promised. Odin! Honir! You've told everyone about the eagle, have you?"

"It's one thing to make a promise," said Odin, "another to keep it. Without Idun and her apples, we'll all grow old – as human beings and giants and dwarfs do, and as you will. Here and now, before all the gods, I swear I will use all my powers against you unless you bring Idun and her apples back to Asgard."

"I may be able to bring her back," Loki said. "If Freyja will lend me her falcon-skin, I can fly to the realm of the frost-giants."

Freyja lowered her eyes. "I've never lent it to anyone," she said.

"There has never been such a need," Odin told her.

So Freyja led Loki to her candlelit hall, unlocked a wooden chest and pulled out her falcon-skin.

Loki looked at Freyja, and he could see how she was already ageing. "Freyja – the most beautiful goddess of all!" he mocked her. "Pah! You're nothing but an old hag. A grey pouch!"

■ ■ ■

The trickster put on the falcon-skin and spread its wings and at once set off for the realm of the frost-giants. He was in luck. There was no one about when he flew into the courtyard of Thiazi's mountain fortress.

Little darts of sleet whizzed around his head, as if each were on some urgent journey. Then hail began to bounce on the paving-stones and off the grey walls.

Still wearing Freyja's falcon-skin, the trickster hurried from room to gloomy room, searching for Idun, and he found her huddled over a smoky fire, cradling her basket of apples.

When she saw Loki, the goddess fearfully covered her eyes.

"Where is he?" Loki demanded. "Thiazi?"

"I trusted you," she said in a low voice.

"Where is he?"

"Fishing."

"On top of a mountain?"

"He and Skadi, his daughter, ski down to a loch every

afternoon, and they fish for our supper." Idun began to sob. "I trusted you, and you deceived me."

"And now I've come to rescue you," Loki told her cheerfully, "so that you can rescue the gods."

The trickster spread his falcon-wings over the crouching goddess; he chanted magic sounds and changed her into a nut. Then he grasped the nut and the basket of apples between his talons, flapped back to the courtyard and set off for Asgard.

Thiazi knew very well that Idun couldn't escape from his fortress on her own because there was a precipice below the walls on all four sides. So when he flew back from fishing, and found no sign of her, he knew what must have happened.

"Flown!" he bellowed. "Flown! Someone must have helped her, and I think I know who."

Once more Thiazi put on his eagle-wings. And as eagles can fly faster than falcons, the nearer Loki got to Asgard, the nearer Thiazi got to Loki.

▪ ▪ ▪

Nothing escaped Odin. With his one piercing eye, he could sit in his high seat, Hlidskjalf, and see whatever was happening in the nine worlds.

And what he saw now, on a bright afternoon, was a golden eagle chasing a falcon all the way up to Asgard.

At once Allfather stepped down and ordered the ageing gods and goddesses and their servants to carry out all the kindling wood from the hearths in their halls.

"Hurry!" he kept calling out. "Hurry! Stack it all up against the outside of our wall."

Before very long, and from a great height, Loki plummeted down just inside the walls, still holding the nut and the basket in his talons.

"Light the kindling!" Odin shouted. "Light it all!"

The dazzling sunlight half-blinded the eagle and he saw the leaping flames too late. He flew straight into them. His wings fanned them and caught fire.

Thiazi fell sideways, screaming, and with their staves the gods finished him off.

Loki swept off Freyja's falcon-skin and met the gods and goddesses as they stumbled back through the gateway. He looked at their bunched and blotchy skin and their bloodshot eyes and he laughed at their weary, wrinkled, milky faces. Then in the cup of his palms he cradled the nut; he bent over it and softly chanted the magic sounds.

There she stood once more. Idun. Supple and smiling and apple-cheeked and trusting. Lightly she stepped from god to goddess to goddess to god, and she offered each one of them a golden apple.

CHOOSING A HUSBAND

Better to be alone than married to a bad man.

High in the mountains where all the frost-giants lived, Skadi prowled from room to room in her father Thiazi's fortress. She prowled and she waited. She waited because, to begin with, there was nothing else she could do.

When, from time to time, she sat down, a frost-gloom shrouded her. In her heart she still hoped; but in her head she already knew her father Thiazi would never come back. She knew she would never again ski down to the loch with him, or catch salmon and pike and trout for their supper.

As it grew dark, the giantess's mind darkened too, above all with hatred for Loki for luring her father back to Asgard. She swore vengeance on all the gods and armed herself for a great journey.

As Skadi approached the rainbow bridge, Heimdall blew his horn by way of warning, but none of the gods relished the thought of spilling more blood. After all, they had just won

back Idun and her apples. They felt at ease with themselves, and with all the beings in the nine worlds.

Quite a number of the gods, including Odin and his son Balder, walked out across the Plain of Ida to meet Skadi.

"How can we settle this feud?" Odin asked the giantess. "We don't want to spill blood. Will you accept gold?"

"No," said Skadi.

Some giantesses were beautiful, and Skadi was one of them, although she always looked rather fierce.

"Well then," said Odin, "what will you take?"

Skadi considered the gods ranged in front of her, several of them the sons of giantesses, and she looked longingly at Balder — the best and sweetest-spoken and most beautiful of them all, his brow as white and unblemished as mayweed, his hair as gold as buttercups.

"A husband," said Skadi. "I'll take a husband."

Odin snorted. "You will, will you?"

"I haven't finished yet," Skadi told him, and when she scowled at Allfather, all the gods shivered. "A husband — and a skinful of laughter."

The gods were ready to accept Skadi's proposal, but cunning Odin added a condition.

"You must choose your husband by

his feet," he told the giantess. "His ankles and feet. And you won't be able to see who he is until you've chosen. I shall make the rest of him, and all the other gods, invisible."

That's what Allfather did. Using magic sounds that he had learned when he hung upside down on the ash tree Yggdrasill, he hid all the gods from Skadi. And the giantess at once chose the most handsome pair of feet she could see, supposing they belonged to the most handsome of the gods.

"Very good!" pronounced Odin. And he made all the gods visible again.

And at once Skadi found herself peering into the kindly eyes and weather-beaten old face of her husband-to-be, Njord. She looked down and saw his shapely and handsome feet.

"No!" she cried.

"Be calm!" said Njord. "I am the god of seafarers and fishermen!"

"I thought you were Balder. I wanted Balder."

Odin smiled. "You couldn't have married Balder in any case," he told Skadi. "He's married to Nanna."

"You've tricked me."

"You've tricked yourself," said Odin.

"Think now!" said Njord. "You could have chosen... You could have chosen—"

"Me!" squeaked a voice. But the voice had no body.

Skadi and all the gods looked around the courtyard but there was no one there.

"Me!" squeaked the voice again.

Then, in the corner of the yard, the gods saw a tangle of knotted rope, and very slowly the rope began to roll towards them.

First the ball of rope began to whinny like a mare, and the gods looked at one another and began to smile. Then it buzzed like a horsefly, and whirred as if it had falcon-wings.

"It's the shape-changer," said Njord. "It's Loki!"

The ball of rope untangled itself, and waved its spindly arms and legs – and there, right in front of their feet, lay Loki the trickster, grinning up at them.

All the gods burst into laughter, and even Skadi gave Loki a grim smile.

The trickster sprang up and landed on Skadi's shoulders, as if he were a monkey, and the giantess was unable to shake him off.

"I'll be more likely to laugh," Skadi told him, "when you tie yourself into such knots you can't undo them. And one day you will."

Odin gazed at Skadi. "You're not easy to please," he remarked. "And yet I'd like to please you."

Allfather burrowed into the pocket of his cloak and carefully took out two marbles – two liquid marbles – and at

once Skadi recognized them.
She clutched her heart, and cried
out in joy and pain.

What colour were they? Difficult to say.
But how well she knew them. Both of them
silver-gold; both palest forget-me-not.

"Look!" proclaimed Odin, and his voice
set all creation ringing.

Then Allfather whirled his right arm and opened his palm and hurled the two marbles into high heaven.

"Two stars!" he cried. "Skadi, for as long as time lasts, you'll look up and see your father's eyes, and he will look down on you, and on all of us."

Skadi wept when she heard Odin's words, but when Njord asked her to accompany him to his great ship-hall, Noatun, the giantess refused and insisted that Njord should come up to her father's hall in the mountains.

"That's too far from the sea," Njord told her.

"The sea is too far from the mountains," Skadi replied.

Njord rubbed his grey beard. "In that case," he said, "we'd better live for nine nights in one place, and then nine in the other."

"My father's hall first," Skadi declared.

Side by side the god of winds and the sea and the snow-shoe giantess climbed into the desolate mountains where everything was frozen and nothing grew, not even pinpoint flowers or wiry yellow grass.

When they came down from Thiazi's hall after nine days, Njord told the other gods, "I loathed it. And worst of all was the howling of the wolves. How I longed to hear swans whooping and the sweet-and-harsh tongues of the sea."

Skadi disliked Noatun just as much. She complained she couldn't sleep because of the mewing of all the gulls at dawn, and the racket coming from the shipyard next to Njord's hall.

So although they remained husband and wife, Njord and Skadi decided to live apart.

Njord remained at Noatun, but beautiful Skadi went back to her father's fortress, and she lived there alone. From time to time people saw her speeding over the slopes on her skis, hunting elk and reindeer and brown bears.

"Restless, wild winds," Odin observed, "and the welling sea. Freezing snow slopes and fistfuls of ice. How can the two of them ever live together?"

THE TREASURES OF THE GODS

Always be cautious and, above all, beware of a thief's sharp wits.

Thor was angry. He stumped from hall to hall calling out for Loki, and as soon as he found him, he held up the squealing trickster by his hair.

Loki didn't wrestle because that would have hurt much more, or even torn his red curls out by the roots. He just dangled from Thor's right hand like a dead fox.

"It was you, wasn't it?" Thor gave him a good shake. "Wasn't it?"

"Just a joke!" whined Loki.

Thor lowered Loki onto the ground and the trickster cautiously reached for the top of his head.

"How did you get into our bedchamber?"

Loki pursed his lips. "I changed myself into a fly. I flew through the keyhole."

"What? With a pair of shears?"

"You were asleep, and your skinning knife was lying beside you," Loki told him.

"You…" growled Thor. "You…" But he couldn't think of a fitting word, even if there was one.

"Just a joke!" Loki whined again. His eyes gleamed, orange flecked with green, and he gave Thor a twisted smile.

"How do you think Sif felt? My own wife! When she woke up and saw all her hair, her sucking—"

"Succulent," Loki corrected him.

"Her succulent hair," said Thor.

"Her gold hair, lying in a pool beside our bed. And when she reached for the top of her head?" Thor clamped his right hand over Loki's head and shook him again.

"No!" squealed Loki.

"Bristles!" blasted Thor. "Stubble! She was appalled! Well, what are you going to do about it?"

"I'll replace Sif's hair," the trickster promised. "I'll find a way."

■ ■ ■

Loki had a plan. He crossed Bifrost and set off for the northern part of Midgard, where the dwarfs lived in potholes and caves.

"Down!" grumbled Loki. "Always down! There's nowhere from Asgard that's not down. Down the trunk of Yggdrasill. Down from the rainbow bridge. Down to Midgard and the dismal ocean and the rock-giants and the frost-giants. Down to Hel, the world beneath the worlds. Always down! Everyone knows it's easier to walk up than down. The worlds are the wrong way up. I need a pair of wings. Yes, like Freyja, with her falcon-wings."

After three days and three nights, the trickster at last reached the north of Midgard, and picked his way down a rocky passage into the cave belonging to the two dwarfs who were the sons of Ivaldi. Son One and Son Two, that's what everyone called them. Their father had been the finest smith of his time.

"Look who's here!" exclaimed Son One.

"My friends!" said Loki, spreading his arms.

"Is that what we are?" Son Two replied. "You only call us friends when you want something."

"If you help me you can help yourselves," Loki told the dwarfs. "Beautiful Sif has lost her hair."

"Lost?" said Son One.

"How?"

Loki sniffed. "I've never heard you can lose your hair unless it falls out or it's cut off," he said. "But how to replace it, that's a different matter. And that's why I've come to you."

"What's in it for us?" Son One asked.

"Gifts of gold from the gods, and the true friendship of Sif and Thor," said Loki. "You know what that would count for. Thor is the thunder god, the strongest god of all, and he'll stand shoulder to shoulder with you." Then Loki began to giggle. "Shoulder..." he gasped. "You, Son Two, you'd have to stand on your brother's shoulders, and even then you wouldn't measure up to Thor's shoulders."

"Very funny," said Son One.

"And then," Loki went on, "you can be sure all the gods and goddesses will be grateful to you. And as if that weren't enough, I, Loki, promise to repay you."

So the dwarfs told Loki to help them build up the fire smouldering in one corner of the cave. Then they put on their leather aprons and laid out all their tools on one end of a trestle-table, and Son One bustled out of the cave and came back with a large lump of gold and a small lump of silver, and set them down next to a block of iron at the other end of the table.

First, the two dwarfs tapped the two lumps as if they were a musical instrument, louder, softer, softer, louder, and as they did so they began to murmur magical words, sounds that Loki had never heard before. The trickster watched while the brothers put the gold and silver into large ladles and held them over the fire until they were molten, and then laid them on two anvils and began to tap them, hammer them…

It grew hot in the cave, and Loki felt so weary after his long journey that he couldn't keep his eyes open. First he closed one eye, then the other, then both at the same time. And when he woke, the most beautiful sheaf of golden hair was hanging over the edge of the trestle-table right in front of him.

Son One smiled. Gently he blew at the sheaf, and the hair trembled and lifted and danced. Then Son Two carefully combed it all back into position, each strand of it.

"There's no point wasting this heat," he said. "We might as well make another gift for the gods while we're about it."

"Or two maybe," his brother agreed.

So while Loki dozed, with metal and magic the sons of Ivaldi fashioned two more wonders – a collapsible ship called *Skidbladnir* and a slender spear called Gungnir, decorated with magic signs all around its point.

"Who are they for?" Loki asked.

"Freyr and Odin," said Son One.

"The ship is silver and it has twenty-six oars," Son Two said.

"This spear," said Son One, "will never miss its mark."

Loki thanked the two dwarfs for their work; he praised them and promised to return with gifts from the gods. Then he draped the sheaf of hair over his right arm and, holding the ship in one hand and the iron spear in the other, he walked out of the cave.

On his way the trickster paused. His orange-and-green eyes gleamed, his thin lips curled, and he turned round and headed down a side passage. At first it was so low that he had to duck, but then it opened into a cool, damp cavern, and just beyond that was the smithy of the dwarf brothers Brokk and Eitri.

The two dwarfs had decorated the lower part of the smithy walls with sheets of gold and silver, and when

they stoked their fire, the whole place gleamed and flashed.

When the brothers saw the three treasures, they hurried towards Loki.

"Look at these treasures," the trickster told them. "Have you ever seen work as fine as this?"

"My own," said Eitri.

Loki smiled. "These treasures were made by the sons of Ivaldi as gifts for the gods. You're not telling me you can make … wonders as fine as these?"

"Finer," boasted Eitri.

"Never!" said Loki. "I'll stake my head on it."

"Your head!" Eitri repeated.

The two brothers eyed each other and nodded. *Let's put an end to Loki and his tricks once and for all,* they thought. So Brokk led Loki into a little alcove with a wrought-iron chair and table in it.

"You wait here," the dwarf told him. "Help yourself to some mead."

The two dwarfs got to work at once.

They piled logs onto their fire and laid a pig's skin on it, they whispered magic sounds, they tap-tapped at a large wedge of silver, and snipped a length of fine gold wire into dozens and dozens of short pieces.

"Pump the bellows!" Eitri told his brother. "Pump the bellows, and keep pumping."

So Brokk pumped, and while he was pumping a horsefly settled for a moment on the back of his right hand and stung him. The dwarf glanced at it and blew it away, but he didn't stop pumping. Not for one moment.

"Right!" declared Eitri. "Pull him out!"

And Brokk pulled out of the flames a silver boar with golden bristles.

"Gullinbursti," said Eitri. "That's his name. We'll give him to Freyr. Come on now, pump the bellows again."

While Brokk was pumping, the same horsefly buzzed round and round the cave and then stung the dwarf on the

neck. Brokk flinched, but he didn't stop pumping, and before long Eitri pulled out of the furnace an arm-ring made of gold.

"Draupnir," Eitri told his brother. "That's its name."

"Draupnir!" said Brokk, looking puzzled. "Dripper? What kind of name is that?"

"You'll see," said Eitri. "Right! We must make this third treasure the greatest of them all."

The two dwarfs heaved up onto the anvil a great hunk of iron, and Eitri stroked it with the tips of his fingers as if it were the most precious metal in the world. He pointed to the bellows.

"I know," sighed Brokk. "Pump, and keep pumping."

"If this fire loses any heat," his brother said, "I'll lose my treasure — the greatest treasure of them all — and we won't be able to claim Loki's head."

Eitri kept turning the lump of iron, and grunting. His face grew purple. And now and then he backed away from the fire and stumped round the smithy, muttering to himself.

Then the dwarf put his head into the alcove to see how Loki was doing, and as he did so the horsefly darted over Eitri's head into the smithy. It aimed straight for Brokk and stung him on one eyelid, and then the other.

"Ow!" yelled Brokk. "Ow!"

The dwarf took his right hand off the handle of the bellows just for a moment so as to wipe the blood out of his eyes, and the horsefly flew back into the alcove and his horn of mead. The trickster had no intention whatsoever of losing his head.

Eitri peered into the heart of the furnace.

"So nearly!" he cried. "So very nearly wrecked."

But then the dwarf pulled from the furnace a marvellous hammer.

"Mjollnir," he announced. "Just look at it. The greatest treasure of all! This is my gift for Thor, and once he holds it, he'll wonder how he ever did without it. It will be his best friend against his greatest enemies."

"The finest hammer ever forged," declared Brokk.

"Even though you took your hand off the bellows," Eitri told him. "Look! That's why the handle is a bit short."

Then the two dwarfs put their heads together, and Eitri revealed to his brother exactly why the boar and the arm-ring and the hammer were so precious.

"Go up to Asgard with Loki," Eitri told him. "Give these gifts to Freyr and Odin and Thor and come back with the trickster's head."

"For once and all," said Brokk.

■ ■ ■

Heimdall blew his ringing horn when he saw Loki and a dwarf, both of them laden, trooping towards the rainbow bridge.

As they approached Gladsheim, Brokk's eyes almost popped out of his head. The outside of the hall was completely covered with a skin of gold.

"Yes," said Loki, "and it's the same inside. Gold from top to bottom. I know! It does make your little smithy look rather shabby."

By the time Loki and Brokk stepped into the hall, most of the gods and goddesses were sitting in their high seats, and the travellers laid their six treasures on a massive oak table in front of them. The trickster had covered the gift for Thor's wife with a linen cloth.

When Loki had checked that Thor and Sif, who was wearing a headscarf to cover her bristly hair, and Freyr and Allfather himself were present, he called out, "Are you all sitting comfortably?"

"Get on with it, Loki," Odin told him.

"Then I'll begin," the trickster said. "My friend Brokk must also have his say."

"At this rate," Odin said, "that won't be until tomorrow."

Brokk put up his right hand. "Let him speak while he can, Allfather."

"Oh?"

"He won't have a tongue for much longer."

Some of the gods smiled and shook their heads.

"You know what dwarfs are like," Loki announced. "Nasty! Their little bodies are misshapen and packed with venom and lust and envy. Have you ever heard of a dwarf who ever did anything, anything at all, that wasn't in his own interest?"

"Has Heimdall summoned us here so you can tell us about the dwarfs?" Odin demanded.

"And that's why," continued Loki, "I'm able to bring you not one treasure, and not three treasures, but six. Six treasures!" Loki opened his arms, as if he were blessing the gods. "All that we ask of you, Odin – you and Freyr and Thor – is to decide whether the three gifts made by Brokk here, Brokk and his brother Eitri, or the gifts made by the sons of Ivaldi, are the more valuable."

"I understand," said Odin. "And if we decide Brokk and Eitri's gifts…"

"We'll have Loki's head!" shrieked the dwarf. "Loki's head. A seventh gift!"

"Well," said Odin, "Loki certainly gets us into great trouble, but he's saved us too. He outwitted the giant mason who built our wall, and he recovered Idun's apples. Yes, he's saved us twice from our great enemies, the giants, so no doubt he can outwit a couple of dwarfs."

"My first gift," said Loki in a level voice, "is for you, Odin. This spear, made by the sons of Ivaldi."

The trickster grasped Gungnir, walked up the stone steps to Odin's high seat and laid it across his open hands.

"It may look much like any other spear," Loki told him. "In fact, it does! But see these magic signs carved around its point? This spear will never, never miss its mark. Odin, your names are Glad of War and Father of Battle. You may want to use this spear to stir up fury and warfare in Midgard, and set warriors and whole armies at each other's throats.

"The second gift made by the sons of Ivaldi," Loki went on, "is this magical ship. She's silver, all silver, except for her wooden oars. Twenty-six, yes. One for each god and each goddess. Believe it or not, she'll expand so that there's room for all of you. And as soon as you hoist the sail, the wind will pick up and you'll be on your way. Not only that, though. This ship comes apart! You can take her to pieces and fold her up so that she can fit into a pouch. This gift is for you, Freyr."

Freyr was so delighted with the ship that he stood up and waved, and all the other gods and goddesses cheered.

"And now," said Loki, "my third gift. It's for you, Sif, and it's why I went down to see the dismal dwarfs in the first place."

Like a conjuror, the trickster gently raised the linen cloth. And when the goddesses and gods, leaning forward in their seats, saw the magic sheaf, the skein, the waterfall of silver-gold hair, they all sighed.

"When Sif puts this to her scalp," Loki told them, "it will take root and grow."

Sif came down the stone steps. She ran the tips of her long fingers over the hair; she held up a few strands between her thumb and forefinger. Then she swept back her scarf and lifted the hair to her head…

There was a shout of joy in Gladsheim.

Sif wept. She laughed at herself for weeping.

"So now, Brokk," said Loki, and he smiled a lopsided smile. "Let's have a look at your gifts, shall we? Though they'll never compare with these wonderful treasures."

"My first gift is for Odin," Brokk began. "It's called Draupnir."

"Speak up!" Honir called out.

"He's doing his best!" said Loki. "Aren't you, Brokk?"

"Draupnir," the dwarf repeated. "Dripper. As you see, it's an arm-ring and it's for you, Odin."

"He wanted the hair!" said Loki. "You wanted the hair, didn't you, Odin?"

The gods and goddesses all laughed.

"Go on, Brokk," Allfather said.

"On every ninth night," the dwarf continued, "this magic arm-ring will drop eight gold rings of its own weight."

Brokk held up the golden ring. "A moon," he said, "with a hole in it. A moon and her hundreds and hundreds of children." Brokk put the ring down on the table and grasped the silver boar, and with an effort he managed to lift it. "Freyr," he called out. "This is Gullinbursti. Golden Bristles. Even if you ride him right down to Hel under the bottom root of Yggdrasill, you'll be able to see where you're going because his bristles shine in the dark. Wherever he runs, he carries his own dazzling light."

"His own light!" exclaimed Freyr, and he shook his head, amazed.

Then Brokk set down the silver boar on the table and heaved the hammer over his shoulder. It almost bent him double. The dwarf staggered up to Thor's seat.

"This is Mjollnir," Brokk told the thunder god. "This hammer will never break, whatever it strikes – metal or stone or wood or flesh or bone. And however far you hurl it, you'll never lose it because it will always fly back to you." Brokk smiled a crafty smile. "And if you ever need to hide it, just cradle it and make the sounds that will shrink it. Then you can tuck it inside your shirt."

Thor could scarcely wait to lay his hands on the hammer. He grasped it and brandished it above his head, and the gods and goddesses in Gladsheim shouted. They all knew that Mjollnir would safeguard them against all the rock-giants and the frost-giants.

Brokk laughed. "It's true, the handle's a bit short," he said, "but that doesn't matter much."

Then Odin, Freyr and Thor conferred, and it took them very little time to decide that Brokk and Eitri had made the more valuable treasures.

"You, Brokk!" Allfather announced. "You and Eitri have won the wager."

"Now give me Loki's head," screeched the dwarf.

The trickster smiled. "My head!

What's the use of my head? I'm not Kvasir, you know."

"Your head!" screamed the dwarf. "Your head, your head, your head, your... That was the bargain."

"I'll tell you what," said Loki. "How about this? I'll give you the weight of my head in gold."

"No!" howled Brokk. "I want your head."

"Catch it, then," Loki yelled. "Catch it if you can."

With that the trickster hopped it, and the dwarf furiously rounded on the gods. "Loki's head. Flesh and blood and bone. That was the bargain. Thor! Thor, help me!"

The god of thunder brandished his new hammer. He stormed out of Gladsheim, and before long he returned with Loki tucked under one arm.

"So be it!" whined Loki. "Brokk can have my head. But he can't have my neck. Not one pinch of it."

The gods laughed. They knew you can't take someone's head without taking part of his neck as well.

"Well," said Brokk, "at least I can stop you talking. Your head's mine and you know it, so to begin with I'm going to sew your lips together."

The dwarf unwound a leather thong no thicker than a shoelace from around his waist, and he drew his knife from his belt. Then he grabbed the trickster and tried to skewer his thin lips with the point of his knife.

That was no good. Loki's lips were so leathery that Brokk couldn't even draw a drop of blood.

Brokk got down onto one knee. He murmured something and – wonder of wonders – the pointed tool that his brother Eitri used for piercing holes lay at his feet.

At once the dwarf seized it and pierced Loki's upper lip and lower lip, and threaded the thong through the holes. He sewed up the trickster's mouth.

Loki stumbled out of Gladsheim. He screwed up his eyes and ripped out the leather thong.

For some while, the gods and goddesses remained in the bright hall, admiring their glorious gifts. They praised Brokk, and assured him that they would always befriend and protect him and Eitri. But before the dwarf set off on his long journey home, Odin told him that Loki had suffered punishment enough.

Brokk looked up at Allfather and his chin jutted out. "No!" he replied. "Loki staked his head, and one day I'll have it."

In the gathering gloom outside Gladsheim, the trickster lurked. He oozed blood and swore to repay Brokk. And he was furious with the ungrateful gods who had repaid him for winning six magic treasures by failing to save him from a foul dwarf.

THOR REGAINS HIS HAMMER

Appearances are often misleading.

When Loki strolled into Thor's hall, Bilskirnir, he was met by a thunderstorm.

"My hammer!" yelled Thor. With both fists he smashed the tabletop, and the plates and utensils sitting on it were so startled they leaped into the air. "Is this your way of taking revenge because Brokk sewed up your lips?"

Loki shook his head.

"Where is it?"

"How should I know?"

"I woke," Thor said, "and looked at Sif's hair shining in the grey-green light, and then I turned over and reached down—"

"And the hammer was gone."

"How do you know?"

"Because you've already told me," said Loki, grinning. "The dwarfs used magic to make it, and only someone who knows magic could have stolen it."

Thor growled.

"I'll help you," said Loki. "I'll ask Freyja."

"Freyja?"

"To lend me her falcon-wings."

So Loki put on Freyja's falcon-wings, whirred out of Asgard and down to Midgard. He beat his way north to the realm of the frost-giants where little streams gurgled and froze between clefts in the rocky ground and the only plants were moss and worts and lichen. The trickster swooped down near the hall belonging to Thrym.

It was a sunny, winter morning and the ruler of the frost-giants was sitting on a capstone of a well, tightening the gold leashes on his pair of hounds.

Loki looped the loop about Thrym's head and landed with a swish and an elegant flourish of his wings.

"Greetings, sky traveller!" exclaimed the frost-giant. He stood up and nonchalantly brushed the snow from the mane of his white stallion. "What news from on high?"

Loki pursed his punctured lips. He narrowed his orange-green eyes at Thrym. "It was you, wasn't it? Where is it? Thor's hammer?"

The giant threw back his block of a head — it looked as if it had been hewn by some woodcarver who had left it half-finished. He bellowed with laughter and was enveloped in a frosty cloud.

"Deep!" he boomed. "Eight miles deep in the frozen earth."

"Ah! I thought as much," groaned Loki. "I thought it must be you. None of the other giants, except the Giant King himself, knows as much magic as you do."

"Eight miles deep," Thrym repeated. "That's where Mjollnir is. And that's where it stays until you bring divine Freyja here to be my bride."

Loki buried his face in his hands.

"On your way, sky traveller," chuckled Thrym.

And the trickster could still hear him as he climbed into the pale blue sky. The sound of the frost-giant's laughter was like the sound of splintering ice.

■ ■ ■

Thor was waiting in the courtyard outside his hall. "Well? Have you found it?"

"Let me unfasten these wings first," Loki panted.

Thor sniffed. "People who sit down often forget what they were going to say. And people who lie down often make things up. Come on – out with it!"

"As I thought, Thrym, ruler of the frost-giants, has used magic to steal Mjollnir. The only way to get it back is by giving him Freyja to be his bride."

"Impossible!" Thor growled, and he glared at Loki under his shaggy red eyebrows.

■ ■ ■

Freyja was sitting in her hall surrounded by her cats, and she was glad to see Thor and Loki.

The trickster politely folded the goddess's falcon-wings, laid them on the chest in the corner of the hall, and thanked her for lending them to him.

"What about the hammer?" Freyja asked.

Loki gave her a twisted smile.

"What?"

"Nothing for nothing," said Loki.

"What do you mean?"

"Thrym, the handsome ruler of the frost-giants, has taken a shine to you." Loki shuffled back a step, gazed at Freyja, and gave an appreciative nod.

"Mmm!" he murmured. "First that giant mason, the one who built our wall. And now Thrym." Loki giggled. "Freyja, she's divine!"

"It's this Thrym, ruler of the frost-giants, who has stolen my hammer," Thor told her. "He's buried it eight miles deep, and says he won't let anyone near it until we bring you down to his hall, ready to marry him."

Freyja stared at Loki. Then at Thor. Then at Loki again. Her face turned maroon.

Then the goddess snorted! The most beautiful of all the goddesses in Asgard snorted.

Freyja's breasts heaved, her neck-muscles bulged, and the glorious choker around her neck burst. The gold links snapped, and all the precious stones in her necklace rolled around her feet.

"Is this some kind of joke?" Freyja bawled. "Get out of my hall!"

■　■　■

That evening, all the gods and goddesses gathered by candlelight in Gladsheim to discuss what to do.

The god of words sat mute; the goddess who heard marriage oaths looked troubled; the god who had married a giantess kept shaking his tousled, unhappy head; the goddess who soothed by day and healed by night looked in pain herself; the god of winds sat deflated; the god of great resolve and long journeys sat at the ready but dumbstruck.

Freyja said nothing.

But then Heimdall, the watchman, got to his feet.

"Speak!" said Odin.

Heimdall smiled. His gold teeth flashed. "Not everyone will like this," he began, "but I've got an idea."

"As long as I get my hammer back," growled Thor.

"Exactly," said Heimdall. "Well, I

suggest—" he flashed his gold teeth at everyone again— "I suggest we dress up Thor as Thrym's bride."

The gods and goddesses began to laugh.

Heimdall held up both his hands. "With proper attention to every detail. Firstly, her linen shift – you know, gathered at the neck, with a nice little brooch to hold it together."

Thor wearing a shift… The goddesses and gods howled.

"And then her gown," Heimdall went on, "a really pretty gown, just coming up to his—"

Then Heimdall started laughing himself, laughing so much that he couldn't get the words out, and once more Gladsheim erupted.

"—h–h–hairy … armpits," gasped Heimdall. "Yes, a gown with straps, and two buckles. And around the bride's … lovely neck, and between her breasts, we must hang her necklace. Thrym will be unable to resist her!"

Many of the gods and goddesses were hugging each other for sheer delight.

"Most inviting!" cried Loki. "Divine!"

"And that's not all," said Heimdall. "The bride will need a bunch of keys rattling at his waist."

"And a veil," cried Idun. "You've forgotten the veil."

"Indeed!" exclaimed Heimdall. "A rather thick one, I'd say."

"And a sweet white cap," Idun added.

"Perfect!" said Heimdall. And with that he sat down and everyone cheered.

Thor slowly got up from his seat and everyone cheered again.

"Never!" said the thunder god in a voice as dark and rasping as a metal file. "A white veil… It's unmanly."

Loki jumped up. "Silence, Thor," he commanded. "Silence!"

"How dare you?" shouted Thor. "How dare you speak to me like that?"

Loki was undeterred. "Unless we regain your hammer," he said, "we'll always be at risk from the frost-giants. They could storm into Asgard. Is that what you want?"

Thor ground his teeth.

"I'll come with you," Loki said. "I'll be your pretty bridesmaid. Your goddesses will have to dress me as well."

Allfather stood up. "Freyja, have your servants pick up all the precious stones and mend the gold links of your necklace! Thor, have your servants harness your goats to your chariot!"

■ ■ ■

When Thrym saw forks of lightning spearing down to Midgard, and heard thunder booming and rattling round the horizon, and then exploding as if it were inside his own head, he knew the gods were bringing Freyja to be his bride.

Scree came clattering down the sides

of mountains and the ruler of the frost-giants shouted for joy.

"Stir your stumps, you oafs," he bellowed at his servants. "Cover the benches with fresh straw, lace it with dried thyme and rosemary." Thrym paced around the hall. "Freyja, Freyja!" he muttered. "My cattle are gold-horned, my oxen black as jet. I've got coffers brimming with precious stones. I've lacked nothing, nothing but you; but wanting you, I've lacked everything."

It was early evening when the two travellers reached the frosty courtyard of Thrym's hall. The ruler of the frost-giants came out himself to welcome them. He couldn't take his eyes off his bride, he ogled her, and instructed his servants to bring bowls of warm water and mutton-fat soap and towels, so that she and her bridesmaid could wash off the grit and grime after their long journey. Then he led Thor, in his bridal veil, to the dining table.

"Food from earth, air and ocean," he announced. "Baked and braised and boiled…"

Thor didn't need asking twice. He ate an entire ox himself, and then devoured eight salmon. The ruler of the giants, sitting next to his bride, could scarcely believe his eyes.

Next, Thor scooped up all the pretty delicacies intended for the bridesmaid and the giantesses, and wolfed them. When some of the crumbs stuck in his throat and he began to cough, he grabbed the horn of mead nearest to hand and slurped it all down. Then he reached out and downed a second and third horn as well.

Thrym was astounded. "Never seen anything like it," he mumbled. "I've never seen a bride with half such an appetite."

Loki was sitting on the other side of the bride, and in a light voice he said, "So fierce is Freyja's longing for you, her passion for you, that she has fasted for the past eight days."

The ruler of the frost-giants burned and shivered. His own desire was so overwhelming that he turned to his bride and grabbed her and lifted up her veil, and he was so shocked he leaped back the whole length of the hall.

"Her eyes!" he yelled. "Red-hot coals. Seething."

"Freyja's longing for you, her passion for you," the bridesmaid told him, "is so fierce that she hasn't slept for the past eight nights."

Thrym's elder sister stood up from her place opposite the bride and walked round the table.

"The time has come," she told the bride, "to give me your dowry. The custom among us frost-giants is for you to give me all the red-gold rings you're wearing on your fingers. And in return I'll give you my love and my loyalty."

"The hammer!" bellowed Thrym. "Bring in the hammer!"

At once two servants left the hall, and before long they staggered back, carrying Mjollnir between them.

Thor's heart lurched. It danced.

"And now the time has come," Thrym announced, "to hallow my bride. The most beautiful, the most hungry, the most passionate of all the goddesses. Place the hammer now between Freyja's knees."

As soon as the two servants had laid Mjollnir between Thor's knees, the thunder god grabbed it. He leaped to his feet, swept off his bridal veil and roared.

Thor swung his hammer and he shattered Thrym's skull.

He swung it again and killed Thrym's elder sister. She had asked Thor for a dowry of gold rings but he gave her ringing iron.

Yes, the thunder god killed all the giants and giantesses gathered in Thrym's frosty grey hall.

And that's how he regained his hammer.

SKIRNIR

There's no sweetness as great as a long-awaited meeting between lover and loved one.

"Your father Njord," said shining Skirnir, Freyr's servant, "has asked me to talk to you."

The god of the Sun and of everything that grows gave a deep sigh. "What now? What does the old man want?"

"Something is wrong with you. Why have you turned your back on us day after day? You haven't eaten a mouthful for days and you've told me you can't sleep. Your father's worried about you."

Freyr sighed again.

"What's wrong?" asked Skirnir. "You can trust me, you know that. You always have, and I always try to do what you want."

"It's true," Freyr admitted. "I walked over to Odin's hall, and there was no one about. I went up to Hlidskjalf…"

Skirnir drew in his breath.

"I did," said Freyr. "I climbed up to Odin's high seat and gazed out all over the worlds."

Skirnir knew better than to keep asking questions. He just wanted to help and please Freyr.

"I looked north into the mountains of Jotunheim." Freyr narrowed his eyes. "And I saw the hall of the frost-giant Gymir. A young woman came out. It was Gerd! Gymir's daughter." Freyr suddenly cried out, and clutched his heart, as if he'd been pierced by an arrow.

"Oh! When she lifted her right arm … she sparkled. The nine worlds were blinded by a flash of icy light. I couldn't bear to look, I couldn't bear not to look. My eyeballs began to burn. Gerd crossed a courtyard and went into her own hall…"

Skirnir sat very still.

"I'm trembling. No one has ever wanted a woman as I want Gerd." Freyr stared at Skirnir. "Yes, my shining friend. It's true, you've always done what I wanted you to do. Will you go now to Jotunheim…"

Skirnir shook his head.

"I want to embrace her, not to threaten her. Will you go on my behalf?"

Skirnir frowned.

"I'm your master. You are my servant."

"I know," Skirnir said unhappily. He knew he would have to go.

"Take my horse — he can see in the dark and gallop through flames. As a reward, I'll give you this magic blade."

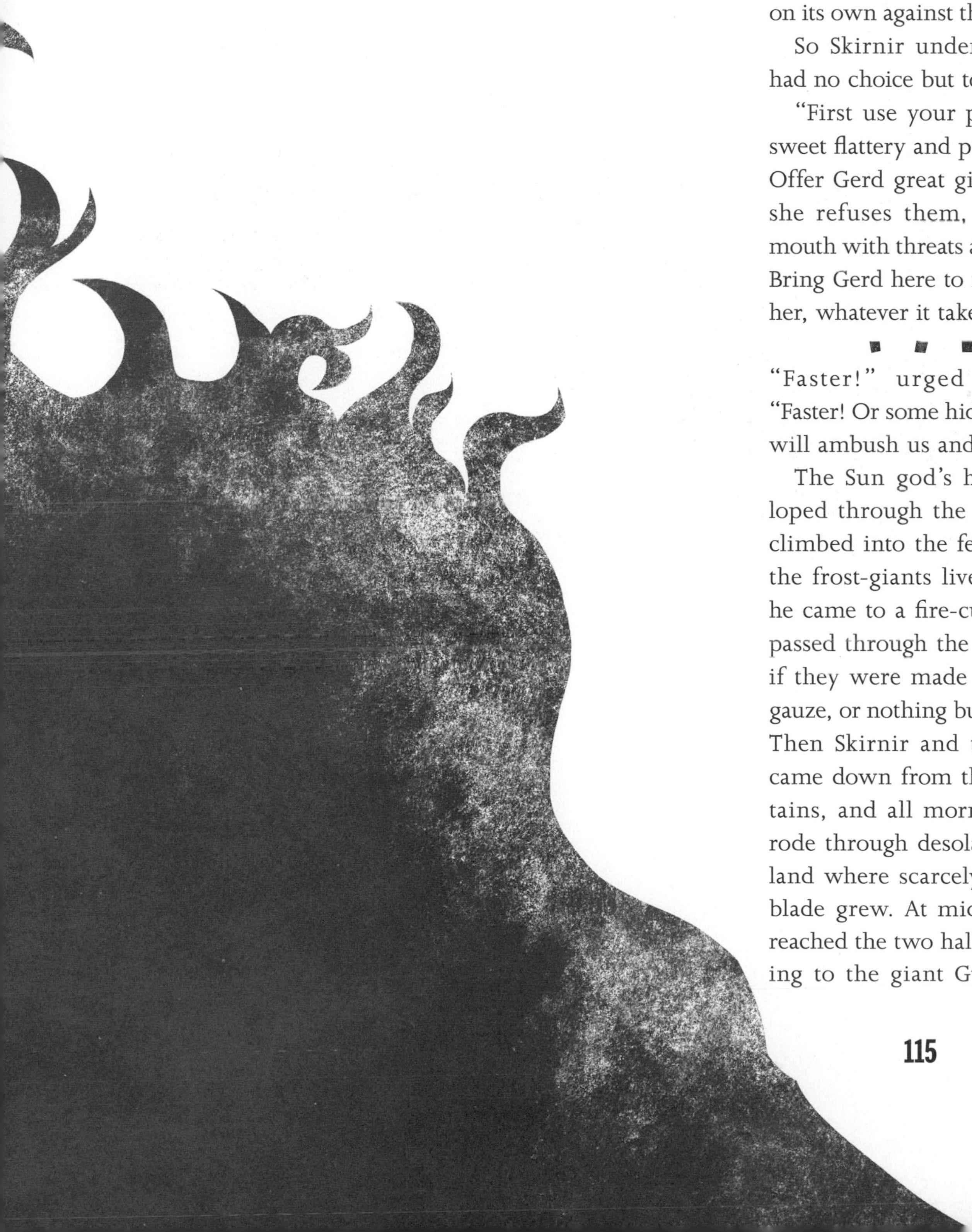

"Your sword!" exclaimed Skirnir, astonished.

"Yes, this sword that can send anyone down to the mouth of Hel, and can fight on its own against the giants."

So Skirnir understood he had no choice but to obey.

"First use your powers of sweet flattery and persuasion. Offer Gerd great gifts. But if she refuses them, fill your mouth with threats and spells. Bring Gerd here to me. Bring her, whatever it takes."

■ ■ ■

"Faster!" urged Skirnir. "Faster! Or some hideous troll will ambush us and eat us."

The Sun god's horse galloped through the night; he climbed into the fells where the frost-giants lived. When he came to a fire-curtain, he passed through the flames as if they were made of flimsy gauze, or nothing but dreams. Then Skirnir and the horse came down from the mountains, and all morning they rode through desolate, gritty land where scarcely a grassblade grew. At midday they reached the two halls belonging to the giant Gymir and

115

his daughter Gerd. A high wooden stockade encircled the hall of the giantess, and a pair of mastiffs half as big as bulls were chained to two posts on either side of the gateway.

Skirnir eyed them and they glared at Skirnir. They began to snarl.

If I try to get in between them, he thought, *they'll bite my head off.*

Freyr's servant trotted right round the stockade twice but he couldn't find any way through it, and he was still puzzling what to do when he spotted a shepherd up on the hillside. He cantered up to him, but the scowling old man neither lifted a hand nor said a word. Skirnir thought it unlikely that a smile had ever softened his expression or quickened his eyes.

"Those hell-hounds down there," said Skirnir. "How can I get past them? What's the way in?"

The shepherd gave Skirnir a stony stare.

"With a message for Gerd," Skirnir added.

"Either," said the shepherd through his bared teeth, "you're about to die, or you're a ghost and dead already." He sniffed. "There's no way in, unless she invites you."

Freyr's messenger looked down at the shepherd. "What's the use of a faint heart?" he said. "Any man who puts his nose out of doors must be fearless."

Gerd was standing at the door of her hall, and she could hear all the rumpus outside – hooves on hard ground, her hounds barking. Then one of her servants told her about her visitor.

"He's just dismounted," she reported, "and now he's letting his horse loose to graze."

"Whoever he is, he's a traveller," Gerd told her. "We must welcome him. Tell him there's a frost-cup of sweet mead awaiting him."

But in her blood, Gerd sensed danger. She wrapped her arms around herself.

As Skirnir crossed the threshold, the seething cold inside Gerd's hall came out to meet him and he gasped.

Then he saw Gerd, and his heart stopped and started again. She was almost twice as tall as he was, and dressed entirely in white – white fur, white wool, white leather, white pearls – and each time she made the least movement, she sparkled and glittered.

Gerd appraised Skirnir. "Are you a light-elf?" she asked. "Or a man from Midgard? One of the Green-and-Gold Gods? Who are you?"

"None of those," Skirnir replied. "But now with my own eyes I see what my master saw – how he couldn't bear to look, and couldn't bear not to look."

"How were you able to ride through the fire-curtain?"

"I'm a servant," Skirnir told her. "That's all I am. A loyal servant who never fails his master." Then he delved into the deep pockets of his cloak, and one by one pulled out eleven golden apples. He reached up and laid them on a table in front of Gerd.

"Payment," he announced, and he paused. "Payment for a promise."

"What promise?"

"I'll pay you with eleven of Idun's apples – eleven apples of youth – if you promise to give yourself now and for ever to my master, Freyr."

Gerd gave Skirnir an icy look. "Not now," she said, "and never! Freyr is the Sun god, the god of green and ripening and gold. I am the guardian of the frozen earth. Never, never will Freyr and I share one bed and live under one roof."

Skirnir tried again. "Freyr has seen you from Odin's high seat, and he does nothing but think of you and dream of you. He can't drink or eat or sleep."

"Never!" Gerd repeated.

Skirnir was unruffled. "Not only these apples," he continued. Again he delved into one of the pockets of his cloak, and then reached up and placed a magnificent gold armband on the table in front of Gerd. "Gerd, this will be yours if you promise yourself to Freyr."

"No!" said Gerd. Her voice was very low, and Skirnir could feel his blood growing sluggish and starting to freeze inside his veins. "My own father has more gold than any other giant. Freyr will never buy me with his bribes."

Skirnir smiled. Then he drew his flashing sword. "You see this? Gerd, unless you do as Freyr asks, I'll hack off your head."

The beautiful giantess stared at the sharp blade. "Not for Freyr or anyone else in the nine worlds will I give way to threats. If, however … if my father finds you here, I'm sure he'll be pleased to cut you to pieces."

Skirnir calmly nodded and went on smiling.

"Your bribes," said Gerd, "your threats, they're nothing to me."

"I know what you do not," Skirnir told her. "Your old

father is doomed to die. He's half-dead already."

Skirnir paused. He let his words ring in Gerd's ears. "If I so much as touch you with this blade," he warned the giantess, "do you know what will happen to you?"

Gerd stiffened.

"I'll send you to the eagle's hill that looks down into Hel, the realm of the dead, and there you'll never meet or talk to anyone alive. You'll be ravenous, Gerd, but whatever you eat will taste filthy. That's how Freyr and all the gods will punish you."

Gerd trembled. Hoar frost cascaded from her face and her hair and lay around her feet. Then the giantess heaved and shook, and her eyes no longer sparkled but began to fill with tears.

She knew that no one who longed for her true love would bribe or threaten or try to spellbind her, as Freyr had done; but she knew too that unless she submitted, she would sentence herself to a living death.

"Drink sweet mead from my frost-cup," she sobbed. "I always thought I would be able to choose for myself. I never … never thought I'd be forced to submit."

Freyr's messenger drank the mead. "Where?" he asked.

"In the forest of Barri," Gerd replied. "So beautiful. So peaceful."

"When?"

"Nine nights from now."

Skirnir gave Gerd a little nod; then he drained the cup of mead and gave the giantess a lingering look, as if he could scarcely bring himself to take his eyes off her, then left her hall. At once he rounded up his horse and galloped back to Asgard.

Freyr ran across his courtyard. He didn't even greet Skirnir. He didn't even allow his servant to dismount, let alone unsaddle his horse.

"Well?" he demanded. "Well?"

"I'm your servant and your friend. I always do what you want."

"Tell me!"

"I flattered her. I offered her gifts. I threatened her. I terrified her."

"And?" cried Freyr.

"Gerd will meet you in the forest of Barri."

"When?"

"Nine nights from now."

"Nine!" cried Freyr, alive to nothing, nothing but the beating of his heart and his own wild desire. "One night is bad and two are worse. How can I bear three? How can I…?"

Days passed.

Nights passed.

And that is how Freyr wooed Gerd, and how the guardian of the frozen earth had to give herself to the god of the Sun.

THOR'S GREAT JOURNEY TO UTGARD

When crossing fjords and mountains,

remember a one-day journey may take ten.

Summer comes late to the north. And it leaves early.

But that first summer morning… It's so blue you believe it will always be blue. Blood quickens in every living body, and the gods in Asgard long to go on great journeys to prove themselves and win greater renown.

"So I'm going to Utgard," announced Thor. "The fortress of the Giant King.

There's no greater adventure than that."

"Then I'm coming with you," Loki said. "Without my wits, you'll be minced meat."

At first light Thor's servants hitched the god's two goats, Gat-Tooth and Tooth-Grinder, to his chariot, and while everyone else in Asgard still slept, even Heimdall, Thor and the trickster rattled over the rainbow bridge and set off across Midgard.

They rode all day and in the evening they came to a farm.

"A very poor place," said Loki.

Indeed it was. The walls were made of earth and rubble, and didn't look as if they had been built so much as somehow grown out of the ground.

"It will be fine as long as we get a square meal," Thor replied.

But although the farmer Egil and his wife were proud and not a little nervous when they recognized who their guests were, and pleased to give them a roof over their heads, the very best they could offer was vegetable pottage. It was all they had.

"Not even a rabbit or two?" asked Thor.

"Or a chicken?" suggested Loki.

The farmer's wife sighed and shook her head.

"All right," said Thor. "I'll kill my two goats."

That's what he did. He slaughtered and skinned them, and the grateful farmer's wife butchered and boiled them.

"As you eat," Thor told Egil and his wife, "be sure to throw the bones back on the skins. Whatever you do, don't break or split the bones." The thunder god rounded on the farmer's son and daughter, Thialfi and Roskva. "You're not listening, are you?" he said.

"Yes," Thialfi said.

"We are," protested Roskva.

But Thialfi was fourteen and growing fast. He was so hungry and it was so long since he had tasted meat that, while Thor was looking the other way, he split the thigh bone of one of the goats and sucked out the marrow.

It was only the next morning, when Thor raised his hammer Mjollnir over the goats' bones and skins to bless them and bring them back to life, that he realized what had happened. When he saw that one of the goats had a lame back leg, the thunder god roared. His eyebrows kept leaping up and down as if they had lives of their own. "Who broke it?" he shouted. "Who split a bone?" Then Thor gripped the handle of his hammer, and Roskva and her parents got down on their knees.

Thialfi, though, stayed on his feet although his whole body was shaking. "Me," he said bravely. "I did."

"Take my land," quavered the farmer. "My farm. Everything. Spare us."

When he saw how terrified they all were, Thor began to calm down. He sniffed. He tousled his red hair.

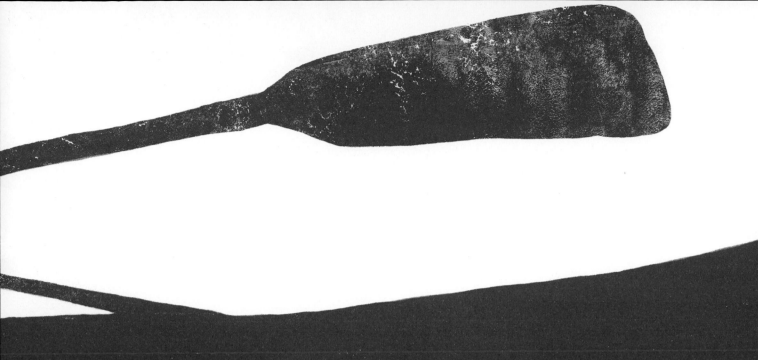

"I'll take Thialfi and Roskva," he said. "We're going to Utgard and I'll take them as my servants."

The farmer lowered his eyes; his wife buried her face in her hands.

Thor left his chariot and Gat-Tooth and Tooth-Grinder in the care of the farmer and his wife, and all day he and Loki and the children walked northward.

"Utgard," asked Roskva. "What is it?"

"Ahead of us," said Loki, "over the ocean, is the realm of the giants."

"I know that," Roskva said. "That's Jotunheim. But what's Utgard?"

"And Utgard is in the middle of Jotunheim," Loki continued. "It's the great fortress where the Giant King lives."

"Not one of the gods has ever visited it," Thor told them.

Loki smiled a twisted smile. "And that's where we're going. You lucky children are going to be able to see it for yourselves."

That evening, the four of them made short work of most of the food and drink that Thor and Loki had brought down from Asgard, and Thialfi kept glancing at the god of thunder, and marvelling at his mass of tousled red hair, his powerful fore-arms, his hammer. And when the four travellers had eaten and were ready to sleep, he made sure that he lay closest to Thor. The waves broke softly on the strand; they slept under the stars.

Up early, Thialfi found a creaky old rowing-boat, just about seaworthy and, strong though he was, it still took Thor all day to pull them across to Jotunheim. Then Thialfi hared off again, here and there and roundabout and into a forest, scouting for some-where safe to sleep.

"He's faster on his feet than anyone in our part of Midgard," Roskva told Thor and Loki proudly.

"The whole place is deserted," Thialfi reported, "but I've found a barn — I think that's what it is — although it's completely open at one end."

Loki and Thor were just as puzzled as Thialfi.

"It's like a kind of hall," said Thor. "An enormous hall."

"We'll have to make do with it," Loki said, "and hope we can find somewhere better tomorrow."

"And hope for something to eat," grumbled Thor. "There's nothing left but crumbs."

The four of them lay down inside the building, near the open end. But all four were woken a few minutes later by a rough, rhythmical noise. A sort of growling and choking.

Thor sat up. "What was that?"

Then the ground began to shudder.

"An earthquake," Roskva cried. "It's an earthquake!"

"Maybe we'll be safer if we go a bit further in," said Loki.

"It's so dark," Roskva said. "Oh! I wish…"

The four of them stumbled deeper into the hall and then Thialfi found a sideroom.

"It's stifling in here," Roskva complained.

"And stale," added Loki.

"All the same," said Thor, "it's much quieter in here, and we'd hear anyone coming. I'll lie in the doorway, and keep hold of my hammer."

So the four of them lay down again, but they didn't sleep at all well because they kept being woken by the same growling and choking, although it was rather more muffled now.

As soon as it began to grow light, Thor stood up, turned his back on the sideroom and strode out of the open end. He saw he was in a forest glade, and in front of him a man was stretched out on the ground. He was ten times as tall as Thor; as tall as a pine tree. The giant was snoring and growling — the very noise that had kept them all awake during the night.

The thunder god scowled. He strapped on the magic belt a giantess had given him long before, and felt strength coursing through him, surging and swelling so that he could scarcely contain it.

Then the giant woke and, huge as he was, he sprang to his feet. Thor was so startled he took a step backward, and lost the chance to hit him on the head with his hammer.

"Uh! Who are you?" growled Thor.

"Skrymir," boomed the giant, and Thor was almost knocked sideways by the blast of foul air from his mouth. He looked down at the thunder god. "There's no need for me to ask you who you are. Red hair, red beard. That hammer. What are you doing here?"

Skrymir's voice was so loud that he woke Loki, Thialfi and Roskva, and before long the three of them crept out.

"Ah!" Skrymir exclaimed. "I see you all slept inside my glove."

Then the giant bent down and picked it up – the vast hall with a stifling, stale sideroom that was the opening for the giant's thumb.

"So where are you heading?" Skrymir asked Thor.

"Utgard. The fortress of the Giant King."

"Utgard! You'd better be careful. You're only small fry, you know."

Thor glared at Skrymir, then he fingered the handle of his hammer, but the giant ignored him.

"Shall we travel together?" he asked. "I'm heading the same way."

"All right," said Thor, rather perplexed by the giant's friendliness.

"Let's eat and drink first then," said Skrymir. And he lowered himself onto the springy turf and opened his sack.

Thor and Loki and Thialfi and Roskva could scarcely wait, and when they'd eaten their own last scraps, they devoured everything Skrymir spread in front of them. Knuckles of boiled pork and braised spare ribs, white cheese, blue cheese, crusty bread...

"Now then," boomed the giant, "you can drop your sack inside mine if you like, and I'll carry them both."

All day the four companions walked through the pine forest, doing their best to keep up with Skrymir. Even Thialfi had difficulty, and for most of the time they were almost out of breath.

At nightfall the giant sat down under an oak tree until they caught up with him.

"Ah!" he called out. "Well, it's another night in the open, I'm afraid. Unless you'd prefer to sleep in my glove!" Skrymir gurgled with laughter, and all the birds in the oak tree flew away, protesting.

"I don't know about you but I'm dog-tired," the giant told Thor. "But if you and your friends are hungry, just help yourselves. There's still plenty left."

With that, Skrymir threw down his sack, stretched out and fell asleep. Two minutes later, he was snoring.

At once Thor grabbed the giant's sack. But although he worked at the metal fasteners with all ten fingers, he was unable to undo them. In fact, the harder he tried, the more stubborn they became. The thunder god couldn't open the sack.

Thor growled, and his stomach rumbled. He realized he was wasting his time and, all at once, he lost his temper, tossed away the sack, strode over to Skrymir and whacked him on the forehead with Mjollnir.

The giant sat up and blinked several times. "What was that?" he asked. "Did a leaf just fall on my forehead?"

Thor shrugged.

"Anyhow, why are you wandering around? Have you had a good supper?"

Thor yawned. "We were just about to call it a day," he pretended. "We're going to sleep, so I'll say goodnight to you."

Then Thor and Loki and the two children lay down under a nearby tree, but none of them was able to sleep. Thialfi and Roskva were too frightened and, what's more, the giant had started to snore again. Thor himself was troubled because his hammer, forged by the dwarfs Brokk and Eitri, had failed him for the first time.

By midnight Thor was enraged. Not even the wheels of his own thunder-chariot made as great a noise as

Skrymir's snoring. He leaped up, whirled his hammer and crashed it against the giant's crown.

Skrymir sat up again. "What now?" he exclaimed. "Did you see an acorn fall on my head? Anyhow, Thor, what are you doing, prowling around in the middle of the night?"

"Something woke me," Thor replied. "There's still time to get some sleep, though."

But the thunder god couldn't sleep. He lay in the dark, vowing that his third blow would finish off the giant once and for all. And as dawn began to break, and Skrymir lay quiet, Thor cautiously made his way over to him. He raised Mjollnir and slammed it into the giant's temple. In fact, he buried the entire head of the hammer in Skrymir's brains.

The giant rubbed his cheek and sat up. "Ach!" he exclaimed. "You again, Thor! Are there any birds up in that tree? I was just waking and think some droppings must have fallen on my face."

Thor was dumbfounded. His hammer had failed him three times, and he couldn't think why.

"Anyhow, it's high time you and your little friends stirred yourselves. Utgard's not far from here."

"Get up, you good-for-nothings!" Thor shouted angrily at Loki and the children.

"I've heard you whispering you've never seen anyone like me," Skrymir told Thor. "Well, I'm far, far taller than you are, but there are plenty of giants at Utgard much bigger than I am, so I'm going to give you a piece of advice. When you get there, don't brag or boast. The Giant King and his followers won't stand for it."

Thor bridled, but what could he do but listen and keep his thoughts to himself?

"If you were sensible," Skrymir told him, "you'd head straight back home. But if you insist on going to Utgard, walk east from here. You'll come to a plain, and then you'll be able to see the stronghold on the far side of it." The giant looked down at Thor. "As for me," he said, and he pointed to the north, "I'm crossing those mountains over there."

Then Skrymir picked up his sack. He slung it over his right shoulder and, without so much as a single friendly word, he stumped off. Long after they had lost sight of him, the four travellers could still hear him crashing through the forest.

"*Small fry! Head straight back home...*" groused Thor. "Insult after insult. Did you hear what he said?"

"He did help you, though," volunteered Roskva. "Carrying your sack for you."

"Only so he could trick us," Thor replied, "when we couldn't open his."

"He shared all that food with us," Thialfi said. "That boiled pork."

Thor rubbed his beard. "Three blows," he muttered. "Those three blows... Somehow he put magic between us. He used some powerful charm to save himself."

For a while the companions stood together in silence.

"Well," said Loki, "I don't suppose any of us are in a great hurry to see him again."

■ ■ ■

Before long, Thor and Loki and the children crossed a large saddleback hill with three rather strange-shaped pits in it. Each pit was almost square, and its sides were precipitous, and one of them was extremely deep.

"Very odd," observed Loki. "I've never seen anything like them before."

When the travellers walked down into the plain, the forbidding walls of Utgard rose up in front of them. They were much higher than the great wall around Asgard or Thor's own hall, Bilskirnir, and were built of grey granite, without even a sprinkle of sparkling mica in it.

True, there was a huge iron-barred gate, but there was no gatekeeper, and although Thor gave the bars a good rattling, he was unable to attract attention. So the thunder god grabbed two of the iron bars, braced himself, and wrenched them apart.

"You ... brute!" said Loki with a cheerful smile.

Thialfi and Roskva looked up at him admiringly.

Then Thor advanced on the hall of the Giant King, and, since the door was open, he walked straight in, followed by Loki, and then by Thialfi and Roskva, both of them feeling very nervous.

128

In the gloom, eased here and there by massive candles sitting in brass candlesticks as large as kegs, they made out dozens of giants and giantesses – all of them very big and some of them vast – lounging on wooden benches lining the two long walls. A few had their feet up on the trestle-tables in front of them.

When they saw the four travellers, the giants began to hoot and hiss and sneer, and a group of young ones whistled at Roskva, and Roskva felt even more nervous than before. She tried to hide behind Thor. But in truth Thor had begun to feel a little nervous himself.

At the far end of the hall, one bull-necked giant was sitting on his own. He was wearing a heavy gold chain, and Thor reckoned he must be the Giant King, so he strode up to him.

"Greetings!" he began.

It was as if Thor hadn't said anything. Almost as if the giant hadn't seen him. His face was expressionless.

"Greetings!" said Thor, much more loudly.

The Giant King looked down his nose. "I'm not deaf!" he said.

Then he slowly reached for his drinking-cup, quaffed some ale, waved Thor and his companions to come forward, took a careful look at each of them and sniffed.

Thor was already growing impatient. "I'd have thought my messengers would have informed me that you were coming," the Giant King said. "You above all! Still, news does travel rather slowly from the wilds."

Thor glared at the Giant King. Then he looked at his jug of ale and moistened his lips. How he longed for a draught.

But the giant wasn't to be hurried. "Or am I wrong? You're not really Thor, the thunder god, are you? You're much smaller than I imagined."

Thor's face turned red. He glowered.

"You're not much more than an urchin, really. An urchin and three tiddlers!"

Thor ground his teeth like his own goat, Tooth-Grinder.

The Giant King sighed. "Well, you must be a lot stronger than you look," he said, "and I do hope you are. I don't allow just anyone to stay here in Utgard, you know. Not unless he excels at some craft, some pastime." The giant took another draught of ale, and gave the four travellers a doubtful look. "Are any of you good at anything?"

Spiteful as he was, Loki was amused at the way in which the Giant King was able to belittle Thor, and yet at the same time he resented it. He felt torn.

"Me!" he exclaimed. "I am. No giant here can eat as fast as I can, and I'm ready to prove it."

The giant opened his saucer-eyes, pushed out his pulpy lips and nodded.

"That would be quite something," he said. "Yes, quite an accomplishment. What did you say your name was?"

"I didn't," replied the trickster.

"Well?"

"Loki."

"Ah!" said the Giant King, and he gave Loki a very careful look. "Loki, yes. The trickster." He pointed to a giant at the far end of the hall. "You, Logi!" he bawled. "Come up here and compete with Loki."

The Giant King spoke to his servants and they brought a long table into the hall, completely covered with pieces of chopped-up meat — ribs and sides and necks and legs and haunches.

Thor hadn't eaten a mouthful since early the day before, and having to look at the food without helping himself was almost more than he could bear.

Then Loki and Logi sat down on chairs at the two ends of the table and began to eat. They bit and chewed and swallowed, each edging his chair along opposite sides of the trencher as he did so. Finally they met in the very middle.

They had both eaten without once looking up, and Loki felt so bloated that he couldn't have managed a mouthful more. But the difference was that although Loki and Logi had both eaten each scrap of flesh and fat, Logi had eaten all the bones and the table as well.

All the giants in the hall shouted and waved.

"Fast," the Giant King told Loki. "Very

fast, Loki. But not fast enough." Then he looked down at Thialfi. "You, boy! What about you?"

"Running," Thialfi said.

"Running?"

"He's quicker than anyone in our part of Midgard," Roskva said. "Aren't you, Thialfi?"

"Is that so?" said the Giant King. "Then I'm sure he'll be as quick as … as quick as…"

"Any giant here," said Loki helpfully. "The whole lot of you!" Then he burped.

So all the giants barged out of the hall, followed by the four travellers, and tramped over to a flat field just outside the wrought-iron gate, the one Thor had wrenched apart.

The Giant King beckoned a young giant. "This is Hugi," he told Thialfi, "and he's almost as young as you. What shall we say? The best of three races?"

When Thialfi and Hugi ran their first race, the young giant gained such a lead that he was able to turn round at the finishing line and take a few steps back towards Thialfi.

The Giant King looked down at Thialfi and growled. "You'll have to do better than that, you know. You must have been saving something for the second race."

Thialfi tried to steady his breath.

"Still, you're fast, I'll say that. I've never seen any human being so fast on his feet."

133

When Thialfi and the young giant ran their second race, Thialfi fell a crossbow shot behind, if not further, and when they competed for the third time, Hugi crossed the finishing line and then ran back to meet gasping Thialfi before he had even reached the halfway mark.

"Fast," said the Giant King. "Very fast, Thialfi. But not fast enough."

So the giants and their guests went back into the hall.

"Now, then," said the Giant King, "it would be wrong to ask the girl what she excels at, she's still too young. But you, Thor, we've all heard how you boast about your prowess, but what does it amount to? Are you really just a windbag?"

The thunder god cleared his throat. "Drinking!" he growled. "Drinking! I'll drink against anyone."

"I thought as much," replied the Giant King, and at once he summoned his cupbearer, and asked him to fill the great drinking-horn.

"This is what we drink from," the Giant King said as the cupbearer carefully placed the brimming horn between Thor's hands. "The best drinkers here can drain it in one draught. Some of us need two, though…"

Thor frowned. The horn did seem a bit on the long side, but he was extremely thirsty.

"But there's no one," the Giant King went on, "no one so pitiful he can't empty it in three draughts."

Thor bent to the horn. He raised it and began to drink. Not sips or mouthfuls but huge noisy gulps. He was quite sure that he'd be able to drain the horn at the first draught.

The thunder god was wrong. He had to stop to take a breath, and when he stared into the horn, the level of ale looked only a little lower than it had to begin with.

"But…" spluttered Thor. "But…"

Loki's eyes gleamed and he rubbed his twisted lips. How he enjoyed seeing Thor humiliated.

"Well, well!" said the Giant King. "No doubt you'll finish it off with your second draught."

At once Thor raised the horn, opened his throat and poured the ale down it. But again his breath failed him, and he had to stop before he choked. When he peered into the horn, he could see there was scarcely less ale than before, though at least he was able to hold it now without spilling any.

"I'd never have believed it," said the Giant King. "Thor! Three draughts! Not only that – your third draught will have to be much the longest if you're to empty this horn."

Thor raised the horn for the third time, but although he drank tremendous gulps, he couldn't tip it right up and drain it.

Angrily, he shoved the horn back at the cupbearer – in fact he tried to flatten his nose with it.

"Oh dear!" sighed the Giant King. "Not at all as I'd imagined. No one here is going to think much of you unless you can win some contest... Is there anything at all that will show you off in a better light?"

"Many things," said Thor in a gruff voice.

Roskva looked anxiously up at Thor.

The Giant King gave him a grim smile. "Many?" he said. "Well, it's scarcely earth-shaking, but young lads here compete with each other in trying to lift up my cat. I'd never have dreamed of suggesting it before, but seeing as you're not as strong as I thought..."

A grey cat sprang down from a ledge in the wall above their heads. He was large, certainly, like all the cats and dogs in Utgard, but not all that much larger than a sheep or a goat.

Thor shrugged. He strode up to the cat and put one brawny arm under him. But when he tried to lift him, the cat simply arched his back.

Then he hissed and spat in Thor's face.

When Thor raised his arm above his head, the cat arched his back further. So the thunder god stood right under the cat's belly, and pushed with both hands; and when he was on his toes,

reaching as high as he could, the grey cat caterwauled and was obliged to lift one front paw.

The Giant King groaned. "Aha! Well, he is rather a large cat, while Thor is a good deal smaller than the youngest lad here. Not much larger than a dwarf!"

His words maddened Thor. "Dwarf!" he shouted. "Dwarf! Let one of your followers come and wrestle with me. Whoever you want. I'm not a dwarf."

"Wrestle! With you?" The Giant King looked down the benches at all the giants in the hall and slowly shook his head. "No!" he said with a contemptuous smile. "It's beneath them. I don't want to insult them."

Thor opened his mouth, threw back his head and howled.

"Wait a moment!" said the Giant King. "I know! You can wrestle with Elli if you want to, my old foster-mother. But I must warn you, I've seen her throw men and giants who look a good deal stronger than you."

Then the Giant King opened his lungs and roared, and before long an old woman hobbled in, leaning heavily on her stick. Her back was rather hunched, and her skin flapped around her wrists and her neck.

Thor was too angry to stand on ceremony. But when he launched himself at the old crone she didn't take a single step backwards, and he could hear the

giants chuckling all around him. Even worse, he was sure he could hear Loki's spiteful laugh.

The thunder god seized the old woman's skinny shoulders and tried to drive her down, but the more pressure he exerted, the firmer she stood. She squinted at Thor (her eyes weren't quite aligned) and grabbed his left arm. Thor threw her off, but then she lunged for his left hand and only let go when Thor slammed his right shoulder against her.

Then Elli caught Thor's left hand again, twisted it and locked it behind his back. The god gasped. He was forced down onto one knee, and all the giants roared with delight.

"Enough!" bawled the Giant King. "Quite enough! You're strong, Thor. Very strong. But not strong enough."

Politely, one of the young giants retrieved Elli's cane and gave it back to her. Then the Giant King thanked his foster-mother and she gave Thor a deadly, freezing stare and stumped out of the hall.

"There's no point in my asking you to wrestle with anyone else here," the Giant King told Thor. "Not if you can't even throw my poor old foster-mother. Anyhow, it's getting late."

Thor felt angry and humiliated and exhausted. He wanted nothing more than to turn his back on Utgard and begin the long journey back to Asgard.

But then, instead of taunting them further or throwing them out of his stronghold, the giant became as hospitable a host as anyone could hope for. He ordered his followers to make room on the benches, and when the four travellers had eaten and drunk as much as they wanted, servants spread out bolsters and pillows for them. Thor and Loki and Thialfi and Roskva lay down and, surrounded by dozens of snoring giants, they soon fell fast asleep.

．　　．　　．

When they woke next morning, Thor and his companions were eager to set off for home, but first the Giant King plied them with food and drink and ensured that his servants filled Thor's sack as well.

"You know the old saying," he reminded them. "If you've got to cross mountains or the sea…"

"We have," said Thialfi. "Both, worse luck."

"If you've got to cross mountains or the sea, make absolutely sure you take enough food."

"On our way here," Roskva told him, "we ran out of food. We had nothing to eat for two days."

The Giant King insisted on accompanying his visitors on the first steps of their long journey. He led them out through the wrecked, wrought-iron gate, and across the green plain.

It wasn't long before the children's spirits began to rise. Loki, however, was rather quiet and thoughtful.

"Well, Thor," the Giant King said, "before I turn back, let me ask you: are you glad you came to Utgard? How do you think things have worked out? And for that matter, have you ever met anyone as powerful as I am?"

The god of thunder knew he had proved how brave he was by risking a visit to Utgard, but as for increasing his renown… He knew that the gods and goddesses were more likely to laugh at him than admire him when they heard what had happened and how he had been worsted by a cat and an old woman.

Thor stared at his feet. "You've got the better of me," he said. "I've come off second best. I can't deny it." The thunder god glanced back at the stronghold. "What's worse, you'll all belittle and badmouth me, and I can't stand that."

"Thor!" said the Giant King. "You listen to me!" It was difficult to say whether he was grimacing or smiling. "Now that we're outside the walls of my stronghold – and you'll never step inside them again if I have any say in it – I'm going to tell you the truth."

Thor looked puzzled. He was uncertain whether the Giant King was making fun of him again.

"You could have destroyed us all," the Giant King told him, "but I used spells. Magic spells."

Loki gave Thor a malicious smile.

"To begin with, I walked out to meet you in the forest. I was Skrymir. You slept in the thumb of my glove!"

Thor frowned.

"I said magic words over my sack and fastened it so you were unable to open it. As for those three blows! If you'd hit me with one of them, you would have brained me. Do you remember that saddleback hill not far from here with three square pits in it? I put that hill between your hammer and my poor head."

Thialfi and Roskva looked up at the Giant King, amazed.

"And those contests! Loki, you ate fast, very fast, not least because you'd never been so hungry in your life, but because Logi, the giant you competed with, was wildfire, and that's why he was able to burn the table as well."

It was easy to see the conflict in the trickster's face: indignation and fierce admiration.

"The trickster tricked," the Giant King told Loki. "You got what you deserved." Then he turned to Thialfi. "You were running races against Hugi," he said, "and Hugi is my own thought. You ran quickly, Thialfi, very quickly, but no one can keep up with the speed of thought."

Thialfi didn't know what to think. He blew out his cheeks and shook his head.

"Ah, Thor!" the Giant King exclaimed. "When you were drinking from the great horn … well, I've never seen such a thing. The other end was in the ocean – and when you get back to it, you'll see just how much you've lowered its level."

"The ocean," repeated Thor. He was dumbfounded.

"As for that cat…"

Thor could feel his pulse quickening and his hot blood racing around his body.

"My companions were terrified when you made him lift one paw. That cat is the Midgard Serpent, Loki's son, lying at the bottom of the ocean encircling Midgard. You hauled him right out of

the water and you held him up high, not far short of the sky."

Thor scowled. He kept screwing up his eyes to banish the red mist in them.

"And then your wrestling… Thor! My foster-mother Elli is old age. There's never been anyone in the nine worlds, and never will be, who's not tripped up by old age, but Elli was only able to force you down onto one knee."

Thor was wild with anger. He was growling and snorting.

Roskva stared at her brother, and Thialfi stared at Roskva. Each was as scared as the other.

Then the Giant King gave Thor such a look that it withered all the grass around him.

"This is where our ways part," he said, "and it'll be much better for us both if you never come anywhere near Utgard again. I'll guard my stronghold. I always will. I'll guard it with magic so you cannot weaken me or defeat me."

Thor gripped the handle of his hammer. He swung it up over his head. But when he brought it crashing down, the ruler of Utgard was no longer there. He had vanished.

The thunder god whirled round towards the granite fortress, intent on levelling the whole place to rubble, and killing each and every giant inside it. But there was no fortress there, not even a single wall: only the wide, beautiful green plain.

No Utgard. No Giant King. It was as if they had never been, and Thor's whole great journey nothing but a waking dream.

THOR GOES  FISHING

Whether or not a man has travelled far, he needs to drink.

While he was in Utgard, Thor had drunk so much that he had lowered the level of the ocean in which Loki's terrifying serpent son writhed and slithered and waited...

But the thunder god hadn't been back in Asgard for long before he felt uncommonly thirsty again. So he decided to go down under the sea to the hall of Aegir, the god of the ocean, and his wife Ran. And his throat was so dry that, far from being civil, he was extremely brusque.

"Brew us more ale, Aegir," he barked. "Brew it here and now, and plenty of it. You're forgetting your duty. There's scarcely a drop left up in Asgard."

Then, to make matters worse, he glared so fiercely at Aegir and Ran that he almost blinded them.

Aegir simply clicked his tongue and sighed, just as the sea herself can sound quite friendly although she's heaving under the surface. "How can I brew sufficient ale for the gods without something to put it in?" he asked.

Thor looked around Aegir and Ran's hall.

The rock walls were pearly and pewter and indigo and grey-green, the colours of ocean, and it was very beautiful. But he could see no container that would hold much more than a keg or two of ale.

"You bring me a cauldron," Aegir told the thunder god, "a big one, and I'll brew you more ale."

"A cauldron," said Thor. He frowned and rubbed his red beard.

Ran smiled, and playfully flicked her drowning-net at the thunder god.

When Thor got back to Asgard, he told the gods what Aegir had said. "And I didn't like the way he said it," he added. "He was uncivil. Almost disdainful."

"My mother, Hlora, is married to the giant Hymir," said Thor's half-brother Tyr, "and he's got a huge cauldron. It's one-mile deep."

"That'll do," said Thor in a husky voice.

"Their hall's a long way, mind. Almost as far as the end of Midgard, and Hymir doesn't like gods. So you'll need cunning as well as strength to outwit him."

"I'll ask Loki to come with me," Thor replied. "Though to tell you the truth, I'm no longer sure whether he's for me or against me. I could see how he liked it when the Giant King taunted me in Utgard, and yet at the same time he didn't like it. He felt torn."

"No," said Tyr, "I'll come with you. I'll be glad to see my mother – I haven't seen her since I put my right hand between Fenrir's jaws. Now, Thor, for a start you must disguise yourself. Make yourself look like a young lad from Midgard."

The first stage of their journey was easy enough, but after Thor had left his chariot and goats in the safekeeping of Thialfi and Roskva's father, the second stage was arduous. First they got caught in a hail-storm – the stones were as large as pebbles – and they had to get down on their haunches with their arms over their heads. Then Thor got blistered feet. And he grumbled so much about being thirsty that Tyr grew rather weary of his company.

But after they'd crossed the Elivagar, the river between Midgard and Jotunheim, their spirits rose. So did the land around them. Wrinkles and ripples quickly rose into ridges, and the travellers made out Hymir's high hall and, just beyond it, the sea.

The gateway into the courtyard was blocked by an old monster with nine hundred heads.

"Good evening, Grandmother," Tyr said.

The monster grunted and made room for them to pass.

"She's harmless," Tyr told Thor.

Inside the hall stood Tyr's own mother Hlora, and at once she took him into her arms. "How long it's been since I saw you," she murmured. "So long. So many days, so many seasons." She closed her eyes. "I've heard about you and Fenrir. My son. My brave son."

Then Tyr introduced Thor to his mother. "Veur," said Tyr. "He's called Veur, and he's a trusty lad. My own doorkeeper."

Tyr's mother was fair-haired, fair-skinned and tall and slender. She wore a gold band around her forehead and gold bracelets on both arms. Thor thought she looked more like a goddess than a giantess, and indeed maybe she was.

Hlora smiled at Thor. "I can see you're puzzled," she said. "It's true, the gods and giants are sworn enemies, but sometimes a god and a giantess, or a giant and a goddess, become lovers, and sometimes a goddess bears a child."

Thor nodded politely and Tyr's mother gave him a long, level, unblinking look. "Veur," she said thoughtfully. "That's who you are, is it?"

Thor lowered his eyes.

"Well, enough of that," said Hlora briskly. "After such a journey, you must both be very thirsty."

Thor looked around him and when he saw Hymir's cauldron, he gasped. It was absolutely enormous. A mile deep.

Then Hlora brought Thor and Tyr very large mugs of ale and while her son was still drinking the first one, Thor had drained ten.

"Now then," said Hlora, "I suspect I know who Veur really is and what you've both come for, and I'll help you if I can. Hymir will be back from hunting before long, and his way of greeting guests…" She paused and grimaced. "Well, it can be rather forceful. He doesn't like gods at all."

Thor braced his shoulders. He kept flexing his fingers and tightening his fists.

"You're both brave, I know that," Tyr's mother said. "Everyone does. But I think you'd do best to hide and let me talk to my husband first. Crawl under that cauldron and hide there."

"I'm not hiding," Thor said at once.

"I don't doubt your bravery," Hlora told him.

"But others would," Thor replied. "They will when they hear I had to hide."

"What's wrong with a little caution?" Tyr asked Thor. "I told you we'd need cunning as well as strength."

Hlora pointed with a knowing smile to the cauldron in the corner of the room. "Hide under that. "Go on!"

So Thor and Tyr crouched under the cauldron. They had to hide for longer than was comfortable, but at last Hymir came in from hunting. His beard clinked and chinked.

Hymir's wife, Hlora, stood up from her place beside the fire. She helped her husband off with his frozen leather boots and reindeer-skin coat. She embraced him. She asked what he'd netted or snared, and praised his skills.

"Well, you've brought back good news," she said, "and good news awaits you. My own son, my only son, Tyr, has come home. Hymir, how long I've waited to see him! So many days, so many seasons."

Hymir looked around the hall and frowned.

"He's brought a friend with him. Veur. A friendly lad from Midgard."

"Where?" the giant boomed. "Where are they?"

"Hiding under the cauldron."

The giant thumped the crossbeam at the far end of the hall with his fist, and it cracked and then collapsed onto the ledge beneath it. The eight large copper kettles sitting on the ledge fell onto the cauldron, and from there to the stone floor. Only the cauldron was unbroken.

On their stomachs, the two gods wriggled out from their hiding-place. They scrambled to their feet and stared up at Hymir, and the giant stared back at them. His eyes glittered.

All the same, Hymir was well aware of the sacred rules of hospitality, and he and Hlora observed them. His servants went out to the pasture above the hall and slaughtered three steers. They lopped off their heads and flayed them, and then they put them into the large cauldron hanging over the fire.

Thor kept peering into the pot, and licking his lips, and by the time the meat was well cooked, he was so famished that he scoffed a whole haunch, and then another one. In fact he ate two whole oxen. Then he thanked Hymir for such a tasty and plentiful meal, and turned in for the night.

Next morning, the giant wasted not one breath in greeting Tyr and Thor or asking whether they had slept well. "If you two are thinking of staying for supper tonight," he informed them, "we'll have to go out hunting. And we'll eat whatever we catch."

"Let's go fishing," Thor suggested. "I could do with some fish after all that meat."

"You're just a slip of a lad," Hymir replied. "If I row us out to the grounds where I usually go, you'll catch cold."

"A good sea breeze," said Thor.

"The smell of salt. There's nothing I like better."

"I'm staying put," Tyr told them. "I'll keep my mother company."

"Right then," said Thor, "all I need is some bait."

Hymir waved an arm. "Go and pick up a few turds," he said. "You know where my oxen graze."

Thor frowned. "Turds?" he repeated.

"Go on, you oxen-eater!" sneered Hymir.

Thor walked up to the pasture and stared at the frozen turds all around him. Then he advanced on the finest black ox in the herd — his name was Heaven-Wrecker — and grabbed the beast by the horns and wrenched them apart. He seized the ox's brawny neck, twisted it and broke it. The thunder god tore off Heaven-Wrecker's head and carried it back to the hall.

"Here's my bait," he announced.

"How dare you?" snarled Hymir. "How dare you? You've slaughtered Heaven-Wrecker, the best ox in my whole herd!"

■　■　■

As soon as they had each tossed back a horn of ale, Thor and Hymir strode down to the sea. They dragged the giant's great barge of a boat across the foreshore, and Thor sat at the pair of oars in the bows while Hymir pushed off. The giant needn't have bothered. Thor's first stroke was so powerful that Hymir lost his footing and it was all he could do to hang on to the stern. Spluttering, he hauled himself in.

"You must be the strongest young man in Midgard," he said.

Thor gave him a grim smile. *I'll show him how strong I am*, he thought.

Then Hymir took the second pair of oars and they made rapid headway.

"You row quite well for a young lad," the giant called out. "This is far enough now. Let's try our luck."

"Already?" said Thor.

"This is where I lay out my line," Hymir told him. "There's plenty of fish: mackerel … herring … plaice."

"Tiddlers!" exclaimed Thor. "I'm not after tiddlers."

The giant shipped his oars, but Thor went on rowing, and he rowed as fast as he could.

"Enough!" the giant shouted. "That's far enough. Any further, and we'll be snapped up by the Midgard Serpent!"

Quickly Hymir secured iron hooks to his lines, and baited them with gristle; he cast them, and almost at once the waves around the boat began to chop and churn, black and silver, and the giant pulled up two hissing whales. With Thor's help, he dragged them over the gunwales, and when they had lumped them into the bow and the stern, the boat sat very low in the water.

"Your turn," said the giant. "Let's see what you can catch."

Thor prepared his tackle with great care. Hymir watched as he knotted a large hook to his thick line, and then jammed the head of the ox Heaven-Wrecker onto the hook.

"Yes," said Thor, "A very tasty morsel!"

Something in the depths of the dark ocean thought so too. It smelt the bait. It gaped and let go of its own tail. Then it started to slither over rock and sand along the sea-bottom, and to rise.

Salt water slapped against the bows of the boat; it kicked up and smacked Thor in the face. All around them, the flint-grey ocean grew more and more agitated.

The thunder god saw his line straighten, he felt it give a violent jerk, and at once tried to haul it in.

"No," yelled Hymir. "Cut the line! Cut the line!"

Around them the waves lashed. Thor and Hymir were drenched, and their boat sat even lower in the water. The waves kept splashing over one of the gunwales.

Thor stood up. He threw off his disguise as a lad from Midgard. He bent his knees, he braced his thighs, his forearms and shoulders, and pulled the monster right up under the keel.

Then the thunder god saw it – the head of the Midgard Serpent with the huge barbed hook stuck in the roof of its mouth. The god glared at the monster and the monster glared back at the god. It spat poison at him.

Thor's feet pressed so hard against the bottom of Hymir's boat that both his legs went right through it. His feet touched the ocean bed.

149

Hymir drew his bait-knife. He slashed and slashed again at Thor's line.

"No!" yelled Thor.

But the giant severed the line and the ghastly monster sank back into the sea.

"You cut my line!" shouted Thor, outraged.

"If I hadn't," the giant said, "it would have been worse for you. I see who you are now, and even you were terrified, Thor."

Because of the hole in the bottom of the boat, and all the water slopping around inside her, not to mention the weight of the whales, it took Thor and the giant rather a long time to row back to the shore.

"Are you going to pull the boat up beyond the tidemark, or drag these two whales back to the hall?" Hymir asked Thor. "Take your pick."

Thor was still furious that the giant had cut his line. He hoicked the boat out of the water. Then he raised the bows so that most of the water drained through the holes he had made with his feet and legs or slopped out over the stern, and he began to pull the boat up the beach, with the whales still inside her.

"Stop!" shouted Hymir.

But Thor didn't stop. He dragged the whole thing – whales and all – down into a wooded glen, up the other side, and all the way back to the giant's hall.

Tyr and his mother Hlora stood ready to welcome Hymir and Thor, but the giant was angry that Thor had pulled his boat so far from the sea. And he was in no doubt that Thor was after his most precious possession – his massive cauldron.

"Many people," Hymir said, "are brawny oarsmen. And many are much less strong than they seem at first. That's even true of Thor, so I've heard."

"You have, have you?" said Thor.

The giant picked up a goblet from the low table in front of the fire.

"See this? This pretty little piece of glass?" Hymir turned it over and over between his calloused hands so that it glistened in the firelight. "I'd only call Thor strong – strong enough to carry a cauldron – if he could smash this goblet."

Thor snatched the goblet from Hymir's hands and hurled it at one of the two stone pillars at the far end of the hall. And what happened? Stone chippings from the pillar rattled against the roof and walls, and on the floor the glass goblet lay unbroken, covered with a heap of rubble.

While the giant stumped down the hall to retrieve it, Hlora quickly took Thor's right arm.

"Throw it straight at Hymir," she whispered. "His head is as hard as granite."

So that's what Thor did. He hurled the glass goblet at Hymir's skull. The giant was unhurt but the goblet shattered, and it fell to the stone floor in smithereens.

The giant stooped and slowly got down onto his knees. He gazed at all the fragments and slivers. He put his huge hands over his face and groaned.

"What begins must also end," he said in a cavernous voice. "Strong as I am, somehow you've turned my strength against me."

Hymir's wife knelt beside her giant husband.

"I know what you want, Thor," the giant muttered. "My cauldron! And I can no longer stop you from taking it."

But when one-handed Tyr tried to lift the vast cauldron, he was only able to rock the rim.

"None of the other gods could rock it with two hands," Thor consoled him. Then the thunder god grabbed the cauldron himself, heaved it up onto one shoulder and strode out of Hymir's hall.

"Goodbye, Grandmother," said Tyr to the monster with nine hundred heads.

The old monster grunted and made room for them to pass.

Before they waded across the Elivagar, Tyr turned around for a last look at his mother's hall, and it was a good thing he did. He saw at least a dozen giants hurrying down the rock slopes after them.

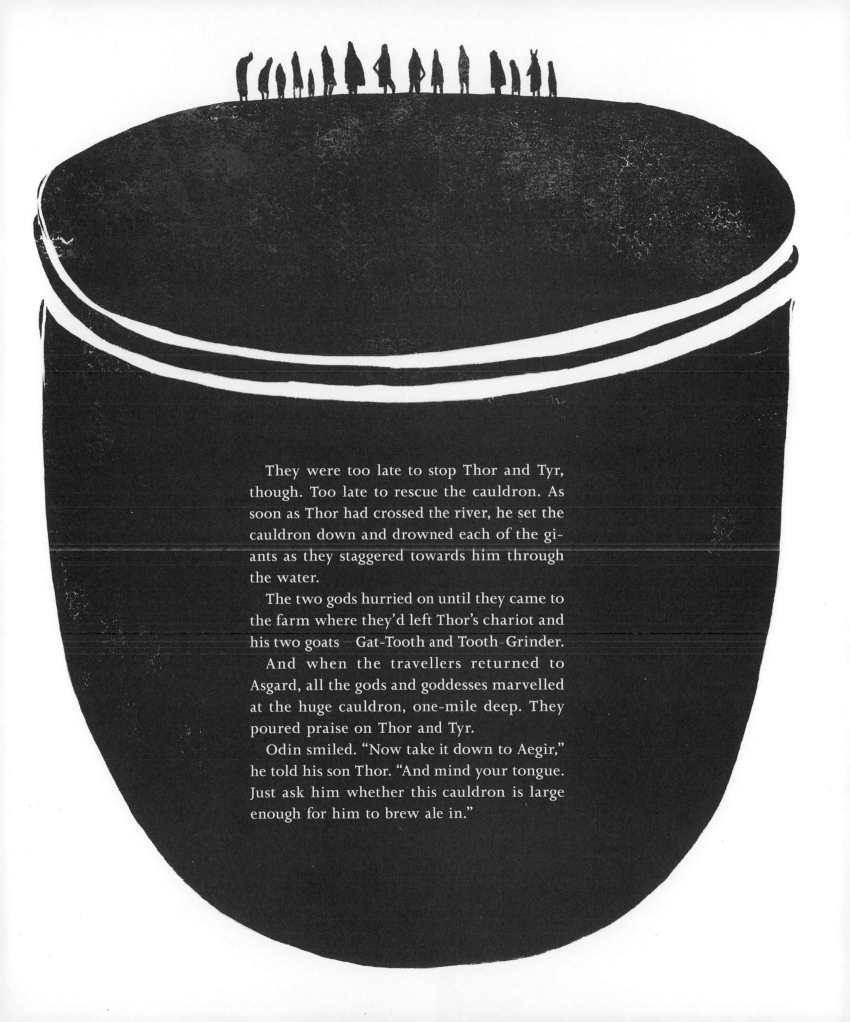

They were too late to stop Thor and Tyr, though. Too late to rescue the cauldron. As soon as Thor had crossed the river, he set the cauldron down and drowned each of the giants as they staggered towards him through the water.

The two gods hurried on until they came to the farm where they'd left Thor's chariot and his two goats — Gat-Tooth and Tooth-Grinder.

And when the travellers returned to Asgard, all the gods and goddesses marvelled at the huge cauldron, one-mile deep. They poured praise on Thor and Tyr.

Odin smiled. "Now take it down to Aegir," he told his son Thor. "And mind your tongue. Just ask him whether this cauldron is large enough for him to brew ale in."

THOR'S DUEL WITH HRUNGNIR

The bird of forgetfulness hovers over mead and steals men's minds.

The Giant King in Utgard may have known more magic than any of his followers, more even than the mason who built the great wall of Asgard and the frost-giant Thrym who stole Thor's hammer, but of all the giants, Hrungnir was the strongest, and he had a three-cornered heart, made of stone.

Hrungnir always delighted in proving himself. He always relished a challenge. And so Odin himself, restless at the end of a long winter, decided to challenge him.

Allfather donned his indigo cloak and tied his floppy wide-brimmed hat. He took his leave of Frigg, his wife, and set off for Jotunheim.

Hrungnir saw Odin and his eight-legged horse Sleipnir approaching when they were still many miles off.

"That's quite a fast horse you've got there," he called out before Odin had even dismounted. "Either he was galloping over water, or he seemed to be. If he wasn't flying, he seemed to be."

"A faster horse than any here in Jotunheim," Odin retorted.

Hrungnir showed his teeth — well, what teeth he had left. "Is that so?"

"It is," said Odin, and he skewered the giant with his one eye. "I'll wager my head on it."

"My Golden Mane, he's twice as fast," Hrungnir boasted. "I bet he is."

"Prove it!" Allfather challenged him. He wheeled Sleipnir round and galloped back the way he had come, and by the time Hrungnir had saddled Golden Mane, Odin had already disappeared.

Hrungnir was almost as slow-witted as Golden Mane was fleet-footed, and he was so intent on the chase that he followed Sleipnir across a dozen fast-flowing, bubbling rivers and around a smoking plain and over the three-strand rainbow and through the gate in the great wall of Asgard before he realized where he was.

Odin had already dismounted, and

set sweating Sleipnir loose to graze after his double-journey. He stood beside the torrent that raced past Valhalla, waiting for Hrungnir.

"That's quite a fast horse you've got there," he called out as soon as the giant arrived. "He must be thirsty, and so must you. Come and drink with me."

Odin and Hrungnir waded across the torrent and Allfather led his guest through the outer gate of Valhalla.

The giant could scarcely believe his eyes. All over the courtyard pairs of well-armed men were fighting each other as if they were on a battlefield. Yelling and grunting, they thrust at each other with swords or spears, they whirled their double-headed axes.

"Yes," said Allfather. "They're all brave warriors who were killed in battle, and this is where they live. The chosen heroes."

"Chosen?"

"My Valkyries choose them on the battlefield and they lead them here."

Hrungnir frowned. "Valkyries?"

"My nine maidens, each as beautiful as the others."

For a few moments, Odin allowed the giant to look at the scene in the courtyard. But although Hrungnir marvelled at the wolf-banners and the dragon-banners and although his blood quickened at the clang and clatter of metal striking metal, he said nothing.

He clenched his jaws. *Sleipnir may be faster than Golden Mane*, he thought, *but I'll prove that I, Hrungnir, am stronger than Odin himself.*

"All these warriors will drink in peace with us this evening," Odin told him. "So will some of the gods."

There were many more warriors in Valhalla, talking and playing board games and drinking, and they all turned round to look at the giant.

Odin raised his right hand. "Hrungnir comes in peace," he called out. "And he comes unarmed. Let him drink in peace and leave in peace."

"I can't," boomed the giant.

"Can't what?" asked Odin.

"Drink!"

"Why not?"

"Who can drink without a horn or a goblet between his hands?"

Odin waved to two of the Valkyries, Shaker and Shrieking, and they came forward with a pair of auroch's horns, filled with ale.

"These are the horns of wild oxen — the ones that Thor uses," Allfather said. "Will they do?"

"Thor!" exclaimed the giant, quickly looking around him.

"When he's here," added Odin.

At this moment, several of the doors to Valhalla swung open, and in walked a whole troop of gods and goddesses, including one-handed Tyr, and Freyja and Sif, and Njord and Bragi, god of

well-woven words, as well as Saga, who used to drink each evening with Odin in her own hall, Sokkvabekk.

But Hrungnir didn't waste his time greeting them. He simply threw back his head, opened his throat and poured the first horn of ale down it. He rubbed his stomach, belched and then did exactly the same with the second horn. The giant drew himself up and glared at the goddesses. "Ha!" he growled. "Never seen a giant before? Who are you two lovelies?"

Allfather answered for them. "This is Freyja," he said. "And Thor's wife, Sif."

Hrungnir ogled them, and tried to rub the stars out of his eyes.

"More ale?" Freyja asked the giant, and she took a third horn out of the hands of one of the Valkyries and offered it to Hrungnir herself.

The giant sank that horn as well, and, when he had gathered his breath, he stared angrily round Valhalla.

"You think it's big?" he demanded.

"What?" asked Odin.

"This hall! You think it's big?"

"Well," said Odin, "it does have five hundred and forty doors."

"Piddling!" shouted the giant. "You think it's big and I say it's small. I'll pick it up and carry it home with me. With all your piff-piffling heroes inside it."

"Really?" said Odin.

"I will!" bellowed the giant. "And azh for … azh for Azhgard—" Hrungnir coughed and then he frowned – "I'll shink it in the shee."

There was plenty of noise in Valhalla then, but Odin simply raised his right hand again.

"Sink it in the sea," Odin said with a smile. "But Hrungnir, we'd all be drowned, wouldn't we?"

"Not Shif," Hrungnir replied. "Not thish one neither – Freyja. I'll take them home with me."

"I see," said Odin, and he winked at Freyja. "Offer our honoured guest more ale," he told her.

"Azh much azh you got," the giant told her. "More than you got. I'll drink Valhalla dry. I'll drink every hall in Azhgard dry."

The gods and warriors were growing weary of Hrungnir's boasts, and they were ready to put an end to them. But this was the moment when one of the doors of Valhalla swung open and the thunder god strode in.

"Home!" shouted Thor. "Home from the east."

Then he saw Hrungnir.

And when Hrungnir saw Thor, he took a step backwards and stumbled.

"What's going on?" Thor called out. "A giant in Valhalla! With Sif at his left elbow, and Freyja pouring ale!"

"Hrungnir comes in peace," Odin told Thor. "Let him drink in peace and leave in peace. I've given him safe conduct."

Thor snorted, and glared at the giant. "You may have walked in," he said. "I'll have you carried out."

Hrungnir hiccupped. Drunk as he was, he still knew he was in great danger. "My zhord," he growled. "My shield."

"What about them?"

"I've left them at home. You're not going to kill me unarmed, are you?"

Thor didn't reply.

"Is that how shtupe-shtupendous Thor has won hizh name?" Hrungnir lurched towards him. "I challenge you. I challenge you, Thor."

"Challenge?" Thor sounded incredulous.

"One againsht one. Meet me at Shtone… Shtone…"

"Stone Fence Wall," Odin said helpfully. "On the border between Asgard and Jotunheim."

"A duel," said Hrungnir. "Yesh or no?"

"No one has ever challenged me to a duel," Thor told him. "I'll be there. You can count on it."

"In sheven dayzh' time," growled the giant. "Right! I'm off, then!" And with that he clumped straight out of Valhalla into the great courtyard. Three of Odin's warriors courteously rounded

up Golden Mane, walked him across the torrent and then pushed and pulled the giant into his saddle.

And without a word of thanks, without a backward look or even a raised hand, Hrungnir galloped away.

■ ◢ ■

There was a rather messy river running alongside Stone Fence Wall.

It was wide and quite shallow, and very swift. Big boulders littered it, and it had a clay bed, so the water always looked milky.

When Hrungnir told the other giants about how he had challenged Thor, they were well pleased at his daring but nervous about how things would turn out.

"What we've got to do," said one giant, "is to scare Thor before the duel begins. We could make a figure out of clay from the river bed at Stone Fence Wall. A rather large one."

"Make him twenty miles tall," another giant said, "so that Thor can see him well before he gets here."

"Thirty," said the first giant, and all the others clapped their hands and slapped their thighs. "And ten miles across his chest from armpit to armpit."

The giants got to work. They dredged the river, waited for the clay to drain, and shaped the most enormous figure. He blotted out the skyline, and thoughtless clouds gathered round his head.

"What are we going to do about his heart?" asked one giant. "No creature in the nine worlds has a heart big enough for him."

So the giants killed a mare, and put her heart into the clay figure, and called him Mist Calf.

"You stay here," they shouted up to him, "and Hrungnir will stand beside you. Got it?"

By way of reply, Mist Calf rumbled, but the giants could see he was rather wobbly on his feet.

Hrungnir, though! His heart was a sharp-edged, three-cornered stone. His head was a stone ball. And his shield was made of stone too.

The giant's only weapon was a massive whetstone – with both hands he grasped it and rested it on one shoulder. He looked exactly what he was: a very ugly customer.

After seven days, Thor swept down from Asgard.

When he reached Midgard, Thor collected his servant, Thialfi, from his father Egil's ramshackle farm. Thialfi climbed into Thor's chariot, and then the thunder god headed straight for Stone Fence Wall, still angry that Hrungnir had been entertained in Valhalla and used his drinking horns and ogled his own wife Sif; and astounded that the giant had dared to challenge him to a duel.

All over Midgard, humans could hear that Thor had left Asgard and was on the warpath. First his thunder circled the whole horizon, round and round, a long muted drum roll. A warning! But then everyone in Midgard swore that the next ear-splitting crack was inside their own skulls. And afterwards, people told each other they had never known such a storm, and never would again.

Not long before they reached the frontier between Midgard and Jotunheim, Thialfi jumped out of the chariot and ran ahead of Thor and his goats.

As soon as he saw the giant standing beside Mist Calf, he yelled, "Hrungnir, are you mad? Your duel will be over before it's begun. Stand on your shield. Thor will attack you from below."

"Below?" boomed thick-witted Hrungnir. "Below?" He frowned, then dropped his shield onto the ground and stood on it.

As for Mist Calf! When he peered down through a window in the clouds, he was so scared that he began to pass water.

Thor whirled his hammer and hurled it straight at Hrungnir. But when the giant saw it, he raised his whetstone and threw it at Mjollnir. In mid-air the two of them collided, and the whetstone shattered into pieces.

One sharp piece pierced Thor's temple. It stuck deep in his head, and Thor fell out of his chariot. He lay face forward on the ground.

Many more fragments of the stone scattered over Jotunheim and Midgard as well, and they became all the whetstone quarries in the world.

After it had smashed the whetstone, Thor's hammer crashed against Hrungnir's skull and smashed it into smithereens. The giant collapsed, stone dead on the stony ground, and one of his huge legs lay across Thor's neck.

Thialfi rounded on Mist Calf. He began to hack and chop at his wobbly legs, and it didn't take him too long to cut

him down. After all, his heart was only a mare's heart, and he was only made of clay.

When Mist Calf toppled and fell, Jotunheim shook as if it had been struck by an earthquake, and all the rock-giants and frost-giants backed off. They retreated to their own halls and farms and feared the worst.

Then Thialfi hurried over to Thor, but his servant was nothing like strong enough to lift Hrungnir's leg. He was only a boy.

"My neck!" groaned Thor. "My head!"

So Thialfi had no choice but to leave Thor and run all the way back across Midgard, cross the rainbow bridge and tell Heimdall what had happened.

All the gods came crowding over the bridge, and most of them made the long journey to Stone Fence Wall, but not one of them was able to shift the giant's leg pinning down Thor.

Last to arrive was Magni, Thor's own younger son by the giantess Iron Cutlass. He was only three years old, but he was already taller and stronger than his brother Modi, and their brawny elder sister, Thrud.

Magni waddled up to his father and grasped Hrungnir's huge leg — it was a good deal longer and thicker than he was. He heaved it up from his father's neck and levered it to one side, and Thor groaned and stood up.

"What a pity you didn't ask me to come with you to begin with," Magni reproached his father.

Thor screwed up his eyes and clutched the piece of the whetstone sticking out of his temple.

"Hrungnir!" said Magni. "I reckon I'd have killed this giant with my bare fists."

Thor bent down and embraced his little son, who didn't even come up to his knees.

"You've made a good start," he said. "If you go on like this, you may grow up to be quite strong."

"Stronger than you," said Magni.

"And I'm going to reward you for releasing me," Thor told Magni. "I'll give you Golden Mane, and he's the fastest horse ever bred in Jotunheim."

"No!" exclaimed Odin. "No!"

Thor frowned.

"That's wrong," Odin said. "You shouldn't be giving a horse like that to the son of a giantess. You should give it to your own father."

"You already have Sleipnir," Thor replied.

■ ■ ■

Thor rode back to his hall, Bilskirnir, with the piece of whetstone still stuck in his head.

As soon as he got there, he sent a messenger to Midgard to ask for old Groa's help — she was the wife of Aurvandil the Brave, and knew more charms and

spells than any other wise woman.

Groa came up over Bifrost. She laid her hands on the top of Thor's head and began to chant, and when the god of thunder felt the pain in his head beginning to ease, he knew the wise woman must be working the whetstone loose.

"Groa!" he said. "Groa! I want to reward you. All the gods will want to reward you."

The wise woman put a finger to her lips. "Your words undo mine," she said. "Wait until the whetstone's out."

But Thor didn't wait. "One month ago," he told Groa, "while I was travelling through Jotunheim, I fell into step with your husband, Aurvandil. He'd been following a pack of white wolves, and strayed much too far from home."

The wise woman lowered her eyes.

"You believe he's dead," said Thor. "I know you do. But he's not. I put your husband into the basket strapped to my back, and waded back across the river between Jotunheim and Midgard."

"Never!" Groa said, and she sniffed.

"I did," said Thor in a gruff voice. "And I'll prove it."

Then he led Groa by the hand out of Bilskirnir. Grey-green dawn light was slowly creeping from the east over Asgard.

Thor pointed up at a very bright star. "That one there," he said. "Have you seen it before?"

Groa shook her head.

"No, of course you haven't! While I was carrying him, one of Aurvandil's toes was sticking out of the basket, and it froze. So I snapped it off and hurled it up into heaven. There it is, Groa, and while all the other stars grow tired and dim at dawn, it will go on shining. From now until the end of time, people will call that star Aurvandil's Toe."

Groa gazed up into the sky, and tears welled in her old eyes.

"Your Aurvandil will be coming back home very soon," Thor told her. "In fact he may get home before you do."

"Oh!" cried Groa, overjoyed. "Oh!"

"Now finish your spells, woman," Thor said. "Work this dratted whetstone out of my head."

Groa frowned.

"Go on, woman!"

The wise woman screwed up her eyes and shook her head.

"Go on!"

But old Groa's head and heart were overflowing with joy at the prospect of her husband's return, and she couldn't remember even one more of her spells and charms.

The thunder god was exasperated. He bellowed at Groa and threw her out. That's why the piece of the whetstone is still stuck in Thor's head, and there's a flash of lightning whenever he grows angry.

OTTER'S RANSOM AND THE GOLD RING

When you visit strangers, keep your tongue under lock and key.

Early one glorious summer morning, Odin and the long-legged god Honir and the trickster Loki set off on a journey to explore the south of Midgard. And by the time the Sun was overhead, they were reclining on a riverbank, chewing the bread and cream cheese and drinking the ale they had brought with them.

"Glory!" exclaimed Loki. He sat bolt upright and pointed.

"What now?" asked Odin.

"Look!"

Odin opened his eye and squinted in the fierce sunlight. He levered himself onto his elbows.

"See him? That otter over there. He's just caught a salmon. It's still jerking."

"Can you see him, Honir?" Odin asked.

"I'm not sure."

"Now why did I think you'd say that?" Loki taunted him. "Have you ever, even once in your life, been sure about anything?"

"Leave Honir alone," Odin told him. "Who would you prefer? A companion who's unsure or one who thinks he knows everything?"

"Neither," said Loki.

The otter took a large mouthful out of the salmon and sat contentedly on the riverbank.

"Did you know," said Honir, "otters always eat with their eyes shut?"

Loki needed no further encouragement. He grasped a round stone the size of his fist, stood up and hurled it at the otter.

The stone hit the otter on the head, and he toppled over backwards, with the salmon still thrashing, still caught between his sharp teeth.

Odin and Honir hurrahed and the three of them hurried over to pick up their kill.

"Stone dead!" brayed Loki. "Two for the price of one."

"Well," said Odin, "wherever we choose to lay down our heads tonight, we're going to be very welcome. Not only are we bringing our own supper with us, we're bringing a feast for our hosts as well."

In high spirits, the three companions continued on their way through Midgard, though as usual Odin and Loki had to stretch their legs to keep up with Honir.

"Why have you got such long legs?" Loki asked him. "Or don't you know?"

"Loki!" said Odin. "I've warned you already. Stop it! Stop taunting Honir."

But Honir took Loki's gibe in good part. "All right, you trickster! What's half good and half evil?" he asked.

When they drew near to a farm, Honir offered to go ahead and ask the owner for lodgings. "Loki looks just as tricky and unreliable as he is," he said, "and you, Odin, you might frighten him!"

The owner Hreidmar was called, and he was a magician as well as a farmer. "With legs like that," he told Honir, "you look like a crane. Or a heron."

"So people say," Honir replied.

"I can't welcome everyone who knocks on my door," Hreidmar said. "We'd soon be paupers. Anyhow, the farm's full already. Two of my sons are here, Fafnir and Regin, as well as my daughters."

"We'll have to sleep on a dew-bed then," Honir said. "Under the stars."

"There's another farm seven miles south," Hreidmar volunteered, "and they'll take you in. With legs as long as yours, it won't take you long to get there."

"Well, that's a great pity," Honir said. "A very great pity. My friends and I have brought our own tasty supper, and there'll be plenty left over."

Hreidmar looked Honir up and down. "How many of you, did you say?"

"I didn't," Honir replied. "Three, and we've walked a long way."

"All right," sighed Hreidmar. "You'd better come in."

"Mmm!" purred Loki after he'd stepped under the lintel into the warm farmhouse. "These late summer evenings. It's getting chilly outside."

Hreidmar stared at the splendid salmon, and sucked his cheeks.

"Very fine, isn't he?" said Loki.

Then Odin stepped in, hiding the otter behind his back.

He greeted the farmer courteously, and with a flourish produced the animal.

"My friend here," he announced, nodding to Loki, "he bagged this beast as well, both with one stone. The otter was holding the salmon between his teeth. What do you think of that?"

Hreidmar stared at the otter. Then he turned his back on the three travellers and without a word walked out of the main room and away down the passage leading to the cowshed.

"What's wrong with him?" asked Odin.

Loki shrugged. "Some people have no manners," he said.

Hreidmar found his sons, Fafnir and Regin, in the cowshed, and at once he told them, "Your brother! Your brother Otter is dead."

Both young men leaped up and sent their milking-stools flying.

"And our guests tonight, they're his murderers."

Hreidmar could scarcely restrain his sons from rushing straight down the passage into the hall and attacking their guests.

"Wait!" he said sharply. "There are only three of us, so we'll have to catch them by surprise. First I'll chant magic sounds to weaken them, and then we'll each take one of them. You, Fafnir—"

"Which one?" asked Fafnir.

"You take the little fellow with hair as red as flame. He's the one who threw the stone. He's wearing strange shoes. Get them off him."

"And me?" asked Regin.

"Take the one who's as tall as a crane," his father told him. "Mine's only got one eye, and a nasty-looking spear. Leave him to me."

As soon as Hreidmar had chanted his spells, the three of them crept down the passage. Then they rushed into the main room, yelling, and overpowered their guests. Fafnir ripped Loki's sky-shoes off his feet, Hreidmar grabbed Odin's spear and they trussed all three of them hand and foot.

"My son!" said Hreidmar – his voice stricken and bitter. "You've killed my son."

"What?" asked Odin.

"I'll kill you. All three of you. You murderers!"

Odin looked up at Hreidmar. "What do you mean – killed your son?"

Hreidmar screwed up his eyes.

"What does he mean?" Odin asked the young men.

"Otter was our brother," Fafnir told him. "During the day, our father changed his shape and he became an otter."

"And he lived on the riverbank," Regin added. "The finest of fishermen."

"Each day he brought us salmon or trout or perch."

"We didn't know about this," said Odin. He tried to sit up but he was bound too tightly.

"If we'd known, do you think I would have killed him?" Loki asked.

"We had no idea," Odin protested. "You must let us pay a ransom for his life. However much you ask, we'll do our best to pay it."

Hreidmar stared down at his three prisoners. Then he turned to Fafnir and Regin. "Carry Otter to your sisters," he said gruffly. "Tell them to flay him and bring me his skin as soon as they can."

The two girls followed their father's orders, weeping as they did so. And when they brought the skin back, Hreidmar reverently laid it in front of the fire.

"You must pack this skin with red gold," the farmer told his guests. "As much as you can fit inside it. And then you must completely cover it with red gold. That is Otter's ransom."

"A high price," said Odin.

"Swear you'll pay it," the farmer said. "All three of you."

So each of the three companions, Odin, Honir and Loki, swore an oath that they would pay it.

"Honour your oaths," the farmer said, "and I'll release you. Break them, and you'll pay with your own lives."

Odin managed to roll on his side and he whispered something to Loki.

"You must allow one of us to go and get the gold," the trickster told Hreidmar. "Release me and keep my two friends here."

So Hreidmar untied him, and Loki sat up and waggled his shoulders and stretched his arms. He stood up. He winked at his two companions. Then Loki laughed right in the farmer's face, and bounced out of the farmhouse.

▪ ▪ ▪

Hreidmar won't lay a finger on Odin or Honir, he thought. *Not while he's waiting for the gold. And as for my two friends, it won't harm them to lie flat on their backs for a while. It won't harm them at all. They think they're so . . . so high and mighty, and this will teach them a lesson.*

First the trickster sauntered across Midgard and went to visit Ran and her husband Aegir in their hall under the sea.

"Oh! I've run all the way," he gasped. "Odin and Honir. . . Oh! I can't stop panting. . . Odin and Honir, they're in danger of their lives. They've been bound hand and foot. Ran, only the net you use to drown human beings can save them."

Loki's need sounded so pressing and

his manner was so charming that he persuaded Ran to lend him her net.

"I'll look after it," Loki promised. "Odin and the gods will reward you."

Then Loki skipped out of the hall, waving the net as if he were catching butterflies, and headed for the realm of the dwarfs.

■ ▰ ▫

When he reached the vast cavern at one of the entrances to the underworld of the dark elves and dwarfs, the trickster paused. He stared at the glistening rock walls, and in the gloom he listened to what he could not see: the splashing and echoing of dripping water. And he began to feel rather guilty at having left his companions captive for so long.

So Loki quickened his step down a narrow passage unlit by candles or glow-worms and, with his arms full of net, he tripped and cracked his head against the rock wall. When he tried to run, he lurched from side to side, and stripped the skin from his knuckles and kneecaps, but at last he stumbled into a chamber with a large pool, lit by a shaft of daylight.

Loki spread out the net. He cast it and waited while it settled and sank. Then he pulled it in. And there, tangled in the net, was a thrashing pike.

The trickster grabbed him by the throat, and at once the pike jerked and tried to bite him, but Loki gave him such a terrible shaking that his teeth loosened in their sockets.

"Change!" he chanted. "Change! Shape-change!"

And that's what the pike did. He changed into a dwarf called Andvari, and, without letting go of him, Loki bit away the webbing and disentangled him from Ran's drowning-net.

Andvari glared up at him. "What do you want?"

Loki twisted his thin lips into a smile. "Gold," he said. "Red gold."

"No."

"Red gold," the trickster repeated.

The dwarf shook his head and croaked.

"Come on!" said Loki, and tightening his grip, he propelled Andvari down a stone passage towards the dwarf's smithy. "Everyone knows you've got a huge hoard of it."

"Never!"

"All of it!" said Loki. "Otherwise, I'll shake you again. Until your neck breaks and your nasty little head comes off."

The dwarf was frightened, and he began to make a pile of all the chunks and nuggets and little knobs of red gold lying around the smithy.

"And those drinking-cups," said the trickster. "And this beautiful comb."

Whining and muttering, Andvari added them to the pile, and then he stowed the gold in two sacks.

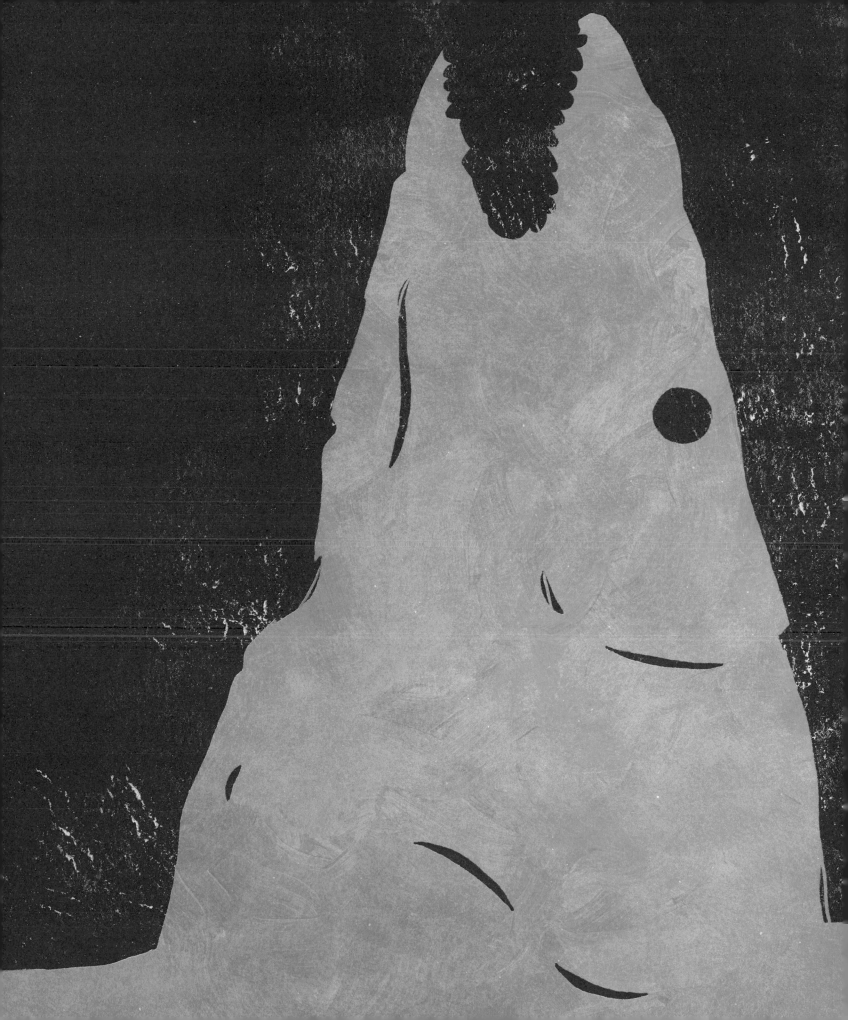

"Is that the whole lot?" Loki asked.

Andvari grunted.

"So what about that ring?"

"No."

"I saw you."

"Let me keep it," said the dwarf.

"Put it in the sack," Loki insisted.

"I can make more gold with it. I'll make you more gold."

"Who needs more?" said Loki scornfully. "Who will ever need any more of your gold, Andvari?"

Then he grabbed the dwarf's right fist. He prised it open and grabbed the gold ring.

How magical it was – quite small, made of delicate interweaving loops and twists that glowed in the firelight of the dwarf's smithy. Loki knew he must have it. He slipped the ring on to his own little finger.

"Take it, then!" screeched the dwarf. "Take the ring, and take my curse on it! That ring will destroy whosoever owns it!"

■ ▮ ■

Lugging the two sacks of red gold behind him, the trickster struggled up out of the rocky underworld, and set off for the magician Hreidmar's farm.

"Why so long?" asked Odin in a hoarse voice.

"Why do you think?" said Loki. "Getting the gold, of course. Two sacks of it. I wasn't picking daisies, you know."

"What's that net for?" Honir asked.

"I thought you'd both be grateful," the trickster said.

The three gods were still bickering when Hreidmar and his two sons walked into the hall – all three had been out on the hillside with their dogs, herding their sheep.

At once Loki tipped out one sackful of red gold, chattering and clinking. And Hreidmar told Fafnir and Regin to release the two captives.

The two gods stood up and cautiously stretched their arms and inspected their raw wrists and stiff ankles.

"You must fill Otter's skin yourself," Loki told Hreidmar. "If we do it, you'll make out we've cheated you."

So the farmer and his sons stuffed Otter's skin until it was packed and plump all over.

Loki opened the strings of the second sack and poured out everything in it, and he held up Otter, snout down, while Odin and Honir stacked the gold around him. The cups and the comb and the nuggets and little knobs, and dozens of slivers and discs – a whole mound of priceless red gold.

Then Odin saw Loki's beautiful twisted little ring, and while the farmer's back was turned, he skimmed it off the trickster and put it on his own little finger.

Hreidmar walked clockwise round the pile of gold. Then he walked round it

again, anticlockwise, and spotted that one whisker was still uncovered.

"Cover this whisker!" he told the three companions. "Unless you cover it with gold, you'll have broken your oaths and you'll pay with your lives."

Loki smirked. He bared his teeth. And very slowly Odin drew the gold ring from his little finger and placed it over the whisker.

"There!" he growled. "We've paid Otter's ransom."

"You have," Otter's father agreed. "You are free to go."

Odin and Honir were still very stiff and sore. Gingerly, they walked over to the door, and Odin reached for his spear Gungnir and Loki put on his shoes.

The trickster stared at Hreidmar, then at Fafnir and then at Regin.

His strange eyes flickered orange and green.

"Take it, then!" he said, with a vicious smile. "Take the ring, and take this curse on it! That ring will destroy whosoever owns it!"

Away they went, the three gods, basking in the summer sunlight.

Honir thought he could hear someone far off, blowing a birch-bark horn.

And then Allfather waved at a flight of wild geese, spreading out across the pale blue sky like a beautiful ragged fan.

He and Honir had been imprisoned for so long that they kept delightedly singling out everyday things – the listening silence that heard and captured each small sound – a mosquito whining, the licking and gurgling of an underground stream.

"How about that?" asked Loki, pointing north. "That hill, smoking, as if there's a dragon inside it?"

The three of them stretched their limbs and laughed, glad to be alive, glad of each other's company.

GEIRROD

Fearlessness is better than a faint heart

when you put your nose out of doors.

"What do you think you're doing?" Freyja demanded.
"No one steps into my hall without my permission."

Loki grinned. "I do," he said. He looked at lovely
Freyja under his orange eyelashes, and then he crouched
and jumped into the air like a jack-in-the-box.

178

"What's wrong with you?" the goddess asked.

"It's the time of year."

"What do you mean?"

"It's spring again, early spring, and I feel cooped up. I need to jump and run. Lend me your falcon-wings."

Freyja shook her head.

"Just lend them to me, Freyja. I'll soon return them – like I did when I borrowed them to bring back Idun and her apples."

"Go away."

"You won't regret it."

Freyja sighed loudly. "Go on, then," she said, and she turned her back on her troublesome visitor. "Take them."

Loki lost no time in escaping from Asgard but he still couldn't escape his own frustration. He flew all the way to Jotunheim and swooped down on the first farm he saw – it belonged to the giant Geirrod and his two daughters, Gjalp and Greip.

Geirrod was sitting at a long table, eating half a dozen roasted partridges, flesh and bones and all. When he looked up, he saw a handsome falcon sitting on the ledge of a high window and peering in.

"Look at that bird," he told one of his servants. "Go and catch him."

The trickster watched while the servant propped up a ladder and climbed it, and then he simply hopped up onto the turf roof.

The servant swore. He climbed to the very top of the swaying ladder and threw himself forward onto the roof, so Loki hopped right up to the chimney hole.

The servant scrambled up to the ridge, tearing away fistfuls of turf as he did so. He was in danger of falling and breaking his neck, but eventually he reached the ridge of the roof and edged towards the falcon.

Then Loki spread his falcon-wings, but he was unable to take off because his two feet had become stuck in the turf. The servant was able to grab the screeching falcon, and Loki knew he was in trouble.

"Bring him in!" shouted Geirrod. "Let's have a look at him. I'll put straps around his legs and train him."

The giant grasped the falcon between his cupped hands. "I thought as much," he growled. He told his daughters to look into the falcon's eyes.

"Green," said Gjalp.

"And orange," Greip said.

"And devious," added the giant. "This isn't a falcon. It's some other kind of being."

"What kind?" asked Greip.

"Exactly," said Geirrod, and he began to squeeze Loki between his calloused hands. "Who are you?" he asked.

The trickster kept his beak shut.

Geirrod squeezed him again, and

Loki could hear his bones cracking and then all the air escaping from his lungs, but he still said not a word.

"All right," growled the giant. "Let's see whether hunger will loosen your tongue."

Geirrod walked over to an enormous pine chest. He dropped the bird into it and slammed down the lid. Then he locked the chest.

So dark. So silent. Silent as a coffin. Loki crouched, and he couldn't even spread his beautiful wings.

The trickster had no way of telling light from dark. He lost count of days. Many times he screeched and many times tapped the inside of the chest with his beak, but either Geirrod and his daughters couldn't hear him, or they chose not to.

Three whole months passed – more than ninety days – before Geirrod unlocked the chest.

"Well?" he asked.

The falcon blinked and blinked again, then jabbed the giant's hand.

"Ah!" said Geirrod. "Another month, then?" He grasped the lid of the chest.

The falcon scuffed and scratched and tried to spread his wings.

"Well?"

"My name is Loki."

The giant's eyes lit up. "Is that so?" he said very slowly. "Loki."

Then the falcon scrambled out of the chest but Geirrod almost flattened him with his right hand.

"Surely you weren't thinking of trying to escape?" the giant said. "Now, Loki, do you want to see bright daylight ever again?"

"No," croaked Loki.

"Yes," said Geirrod. "Of course you do. I'll make you an offer. If you swear an oath to bring me Thor, our greatest enemy, without his hammer, I'll spare your miserable life."

Loki stared gloomily into his coffin.

Almost gently at first, but then with greater and greater force, the giant began his terrible clamping and constricting and crushing again.

"I swear," gasped Loki.

So Geirrod allowed the falcon out of the chest, and Gjalp and Greip fed him. But because he hadn't eaten a morsel for three months, every mouthful of food went straight through him.

"On your way!" said Geirrod. "You filthy, loathsome…"

Loki spread his falcon-wings. He skimmed over Midgard and it was bright with waking wildflowers and scented with clover and hawthorn.

■ ▰ ■

Early June. There's no better time for travelling, and there was still no one Thor liked as a travelling companion so much as Loki.

True, the trickster was as flighty as

an eider-duck and as slippery as a grass snake – and true again, he had laughed spitefully in Thor's face when he had been outwitted by the Giant King – but even though Thor no longer fully trusted Loki, the thunder god relished his quick wit and sharp tongue, so unlike his own.

So when Loki had fully recovered from his long imprisonment and suggested that they should spend a couple of peaceful days exploring a remote part of Midgard, Thor readily agreed.

"By all means," he said. "Days just for ourselves. Where have you been, anyhow? I've haven't seen you at all during the last three months."

As soon as they set out, Loki was full of the joys of the spring he had missed! He talked and talked, he laughed, he whistled; the daylight faded, and Thor suspected nothing.

"I'll tell you what," said Loki. "It's only a hop and a skip from here to Grid's farm. How about we pay her a visit?"

"Grid," said Thor. "Yes, she may be a giantess, but I do like her."

Loki snickered. "Not half as much as your father Odin does," he said. "She's the mother of your half-brother Vidar, the silent god. Anyhow, she'll give us food and shelter."

Thor grunted.

"And from Grid's farm," Loki went on, "it's only a skip and a jump to Geirrod's."

"Who?"

"Geirrod."

"Never heard of him."

"A rock-giant. A rather ugly one. But he's got two gorgeous daughters." Loki shook his head and sighed. "You won't think much of him, but you certainly won't regret meeting them. We can call in on our way back to Asgard."

"All right, then," said Thor. "There's no harm in that."

■ ■ ■

"No harm! There's every harm!" the giantess Grid warned Thor later that evening. "Are you blind? Can't you see how malicious Loki is becoming? And shall I tell you the truth about Geirrod?"

She looked down at Loki, lying between them, softly snoring.

"He's not much good at holding his drink," Thor told her, and he hiccupped.

"You've drunk a skinful yourself," said Grid. "Now listen to me. Geirrod would like to grind you gods, grind you and mash you, and there's no god he hates as much as the one who killed Hrungnir."

"But…" said Thor, and he tried to blink the ale-mist out of his head. "But that was me."

"Exactly!" said Grid. "He'll give you a warm welcome, you can count on that. Red-hot, in fact."

Thor rumbled.

"You've got your hammer?"

Thor reached for his belt but then he remembered… "But Loki told me…"

"What?" demanded the giantess. "What did he tell you?"

"Um … we'd have two days just for ourselves. Peaceful days. And, um … two gorgeous daughters."

"You can't go to Geirrod's farm un-armed. In the name of your father, Odin, I'll lend you my weapons. My iron gauntlets. My unbreakable staff. Take them with you."

Thor put his hands to his head and groaned. He settled himself into the straw beside Loki, and fell asleep.

When the trickster woke and saw Grid's weapons, he wondered what the giantess and Thor had said to each other while he lay asleep. And when Thor woke, he wondered just how much Loki knew about Geirrod.

But once they were on their way, Thor and Loki were soon spring-heeling over the bouncy summer turf, and before long they came to the bank of a broad, rusty river.

"Look at the water," said Thor. "Brown. Almost red."

"It's all the iron in it," Loki told him.

"And look how rapid it is. It's run-ning away with itself."

Thor waded in. He prodded the river bed and picked out his way with Grid's staff, but the river soon became so deep that Loki had to ride on Thor's back.

"There's magic in this river," Thor called out. "My hips … armpits … the water's over my shoulders. It's rising, and rising fast."

Loki put his arms round Thor's neck.

But at that moment the thunder god lost his footing on the slippery river bed, and at once the torrent swept him downstream with screeching Loki still clinging to his back.

Twice Thor grabbed at slimy saplings growing in the river but they were lean and flimsy and he uprooted them. Then he grasped a rowan tree and the rowan held firm. The god recovered his footing and, soaked from head to toe, he and Loki stumbled through the stony shallows onto the far bank.

"That rowan saved our lives," Thor told Loki. "You know what people say?"

"What?" asked Loki.

Thor scratched his head. "Something about rowan and red thread."

"That's right," said Loki. "Rowan and red threads guard you against witches and giants."

When Loki saw Geirrod's farm, it made him feel ill – he remembered the terrible squeezing, the ache of his hunger, the silence and darkness of the coffin-chest. But then he thought of how the giant would run him to ground and tear him into pieces if he broke his oath. Not only that. He relished the prospect of causing further trouble for the gods, and then he hated himself for doing so.

"What is it?" asked Thor.

The trickster's eyes gleamed. "I'm my enemy's friend," he said, "and my friend's enemy. I'm really my own worst enemy."

"You'll tie your tongue in knots one day," said Thor.

After Thor and Loki had crossed a clear, bubbling stream, they reached the farm, and there they were accosted by the same servant who had risked his life to climb up onto the roof and capture Loki when he was wearing Freyja's falcon-wings.

"Geirrod's away," he informed them. "He told me that if guests arrived, I should show you to your room."

"Why?" asked Thor. "Is he expecting us?" The god of thunder looked suspiciously at Loki and narrowed his eyes. His shaggy red eyebrows twitched, but the trickster simply shrugged and then turned away.

To Thor's surprise, the servant led them back across the courtyard and then through the pigsty to a scruffy paddock and a goat-shed.

"These are your quarters," said the servant, and with that he walked out and slammed the ill-fitting door behind him.

Thor inspected the shed, but in truth there was nothing much to see. A single chair for the goatherd. A bristle of straw to sleep on. A sticky mud floor. Rafters and a large crossbeam. Hundreds of cobwebs.

The god of thunder glared at Loki, but the trickster raised his shoulder blades and his eyebrows, and shook his head. "I'm just as bewildered as you are," he said.

"We could be back in Asgard and drinking in my hall by now," said Thor. "Where are those daughters?"

Loki sighed loudly. "I'm going to wash myself in that stream," he said. "We're both caked in mud."

"And then we'll find food and drink," Thor added. "It had better be good."

Thor lumped himself into the chair. He felt very weary, and annoyed with Loki, and annoyed with Geirrod for his dreadful hospitality. Then he closed his hands round Grid's shapely staff. Those lovely daughters... He breathed deeply and closed his eyes.

Thor had a dream. He was crossing that rusty river again. Then he slipped and lost his footing. He was flailing, he was floating...

The thunder god opened his eyes. At once he saw that he and his chair were rising towards the rafters and the hefty crossbeam, and realized he was in danger of being driven against it.

Thor pushed so fiercely against the crossbeam that whatever was beneath the chair, pushing him up, was unable to lift him any further. And then, when the god's head was only inches from being squashed, whatever it was

pushing him from below could resist no longer, and gave way and collapsed.

There was screaming in the goat-shed as Geirrod's two gorgeous daughters, Gjalp and Greip, were crushed under the weight of the chair with Thor sitting in it.

Loki heard their howling as he hurried back from the stream, and then all the goats and pigs and other beasts on Geirrod's farm joined in — they bleated and snorted and whinnied and brayed. As for the girls, they moaned. Their arms and legs were broken, their ribcages smashed, their spines were snapped.

While Loki was standing on the threshold of the goat-shed, staring at the carnage and trying to work out what had happened, Geirrod's servant came up behind him.

"My master's back," he announced. "He's looking forward to welcoming you. He says he's got a game or two he'd like to play with Thor."

Thor stood up. He stepped over the bodies of Gjalp and Greip, and followed Loki and the servant out of the shed.

Then he clamped his hands against the trickster's cheeks and glared at him. "You knew about this," he said. "You did, didn't you?"

"No," said Loki. His orange-green eyes flickered.

"*Only a skip and a jump to Geirrod's ... two*

186

gorgeous daughters ... you certainly won't regret meeting them. You've tricked me."

Loki shook his head, and Thor shook Loki. "Yes, you have. I know you have. I'll deal with you later."

But Thor hadn't forgotten the other gift the giantess Grid had given him. "Before I step into the hall," he said, "I'm going to arm myself." Then he put on Grid's iron gauntlets.

Grim-faced, the thunder god stepped under the lintel into Geirrod's hall, followed by Loki, and at once Geirrod's servant bolted the door.

Loki looked around him, surprised.

In place of the massive eating table, the coffin-chest and the hearth, there was now a trench stretching right down the middle of the hall, full of blazing coals. The air was so hot it quivered.

Geirrod was standing at the far end, and at once he stepped forward, right hand outstretched.

"Welcome, Thor!" he bawled.

The giant picked up a pair of tongs. He stooped, grasped a glowing iron ball, and hurled it straight at the thunder god.

Thor caught it! In his iron gauntlets he caught it. He growled and all Geirrod's servants dived into the corners, and

Geirrod retreated behind one of the iron pillars at the far end of the hall.

The god of thunder glared at the iron pillar. He opened his mouth and roared, he roared and hurled the ball straight back at the pillar.

Between his splayed fingers, Loki watched as red-hot iron met cold iron, and the ball punched a hole right through the pillar. It punched a hole through Geirrod's paunch. Then it punctured the stone wall and lay, whistling, on the earth bank outside.

Loki smiled and he shivered. He unbolted the hall door as quietly as he could. Hating himself and afraid of Thor, he slipped away into the night.

Geirrod's body was like a pig's bladder with a leak in it. He hissed, he gurgled, he sagged. He lurched and then he fell over sideways.

With Grid's magic staff, Thor smashed the skulls of all Geirrod's servants. Then he too stepped out of the oven-hot hall into the cool air. Grimacing, he stumped away.

And that night, under the watchful eyes of the stars, the thunder god and the trickster each walked back to Asgard on his own.

ALVIS OUTWITTED

What you and you alone know – there's nothing better.

It was early evening when Alvis, the pale-nosed dwarf, reached up and grasped the latch. He pushed with both hands, and put his head round the door of Thor's hall, Bilskirnir.

"Anyone at home?" he called out, and his reedy voice answered him from the stone walls and high rafters.

Down at the far end of the hall, someone was tipping back a horn of ale.

"Don't mind me!" piped the dwarf. "I've only been walking for three days and two nights to get here. Who are you, anyway?"

The someone banged down his drinking-horn on a table half as long as the hall. "My name? Thor!" he growled. "The god of thunder."

"Ooh!" exclaimed the dwarf.

"And who are you, you miserable, pale-nosed creature? Where have you come from? Are all your friends corpses?"

The dwarf drew himself up and dusted himself down. "Alvis," he replied. "Alvis is the name. And I've tramped all the way from the far side of Midgard to claim my reward."

"Reward for what?"

"Setting stones in gold rings, sharpening weapons, making a drill — all kinds of things for you gods."

"And what's the reward?"

"Your daughter Thrud."

Thor slammed the flat of his right hand against the table.

"As my bride," the dwarf added.

"Never!"

"It was sworn."

"Sworn? Who swore it?"

The dwarf waved his hands airily. "Orange eyes. Green flecks. A light, little fellow."

The god of thunder glared at Alvis. "Thrud doesn't belong to Loki! She's my daughter, and no one but I will decide whom she is to marry."

"You gods can't break an oath," Alvis said. "It's sacred."

"Loki's not a god," Thor replied, angrily. "He may live with us but he's the son of two giants, and as evil as he is good." He kept dragging his fingers through his bushy red beard. "The fate of my daughter matters more to me than any oath."

"You must honour it. You know that whoever lives in Asgard and swears an oath swears it in the name of all the gods," Alvis reminded him. "I know that. There's nothing in the nine worlds that I do not know."

"There is nothing … you do not know," Thor repeated. "Nothing in the nine worlds?" The thunder god gave the dwarf one long look. "All right, Alvis! If that's so, and if you can answer all my questions, I shall be obliged to honour the oath, and you can claim Thrud."

Alvis shook his head.

"What?" demanded Thor.

"You can ask me as many questions as you like before the Sun rises. But as you know, we dwarfs have to hide and stop the Sun from seeing us or else we turn to stone."

Thor growled and nodded.

"Fair-skinned," said Alvis, and he smiled a pallid little smile. "Shining. Shapely. Strong. Those are my names for Thrud. Where is she, anyhow?"

Thor waved away Alvis's question, sat down on a bench and gestured to the dwarf to do the same. But when Alvis sat down opposite him, he couldn't see over the tabletop, so he perched on the edge of the table.

"Well now, Alvis, I'll ask you questions about naming – all the names my father Odin taught me when I was very young, no older than Magni, my own little son. Yes, all the names I've never forgotten. What are the names for the land beneath our feet, and stretching to the far distance, in each of the worlds?"

"Mmm!" murmured the dwarf, as if he scarcely knew. "Well, humans call it Earth and the Warrior Gods call it the Field, the Green-and-Gold Gods call it the Ways. The giants say Evergreen and the greatest of the gods call it Clay."

"Right, Alvis, what are the names for the sky in each and every world?"

"Humans call it Heaven and the Warrior Gods say the Height. The

191

Green-and-Gold Gods say Wind-Weaver. The giants, they say Top World, the elves say Lovely Roof and we dwarfs say Dripping Hall."

"Dripping Hall, eh?" repeated Thor. "What about the Moon, then?"

"Moon," repeated the dwarf. "That's what the humans call him. But you gods sometimes say Mock Sun. Down in Hel he's called Whirling Wheel. The giants say Traveller, the elves Time-Teller, and we dwarfs say the Gleamer."

"And the Sun?" asked Thor.

"The humans call her Sun, the gods sometimes say Orb, the giants Ever Bright, the elves Shining Wheel. We dwarfs, we say Dvalin's Delight."

"Oh?" asked Thor. "Who was he? A dwarf?"

"He was," said Alvis in a bitter voice, "and a warning to us all."

"A warning?"

"The rising Sun saw him."

Thor shrugged. "What about men and women in Midgard? What do they call the Sun?"

"All-Glowing," said Alvis.

"True," said Thor, and he scratched his right ear. "You know more than I thought you would."

"I claim my reward," screeched the dwarf.

Thor looked down at his visitor and smiled. "Claim your reward? I've scarcely begun. What are the names for the clouds that bring us rain?"

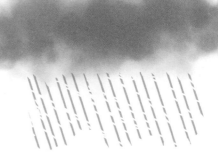

"Humans say Clouds. Warrior Gods say Chance of Showers and the Green-and-Gold Gods say Wind Kites. Hopes of a Soaking, that's what the giants say, and the elves say High and Mighty. I know what they're called down in Hel too: Helmets of Secrets."

"What's the name for the wind, then, the wind hurrying and scurrying to and fro, further than any traveller?"

"Humans say Wind," Alvis replied. "The gods say Waverer and the most

holy gods, you and Odin and Freyr and Freyja, you say Neigher. Wailer, say the giants. Roaring Traveller, the elves say. And down in Hel it's Blustering Blast."

"What about its opposite?" asked Thor. "When the wind drops and the air is still, are there names for that?"

"Humans say Calm. Warrior Gods say Quiet and the Green-and-Gold Gods say Wind Hush. The giants call it Sultry, the elves Stillness, and we dwarfs say Shelter."

"All right, Alvis. What are the names for the ocean that we all sail on?"

"Well," said the dwarf, "humans say Sea and Warrior Gods say Level and the Green-and-Gold Gods say Waves. Eel Home, that's what the giants call it, and the elves—" Alvis screwed up his face— "the elves say Drink-Stuff and we dwarfs say the Deep."

"Fire!" exclaimed Thor. "Fire that we light in our hearths. What are the names for that?"

"Humans say Fire. The Warrior Gods say Flame and the Green-and-Gold Gods say Wave. What the giants say is Hungry Biter and we dwarfs say Burner. Down in Hel it's called the Hasty."

"Well then, Alvis," said the thunder god, "what about wood, wood that grows for the use of all creation?"

"Yes," the dwarf replied. "Humans say Wood, Warrior Gods say Mane of the Field and the Green-and-Gold Gods say Wand. The giants say Fuel and the elves Lovely-Limbed. Down in Hel, it's Seaweed of the Hills."

"Hmmm!" growled Thor. Alvis knew much more than he had expected, but the thunder god had no intention whatsoever of allowing him to claim his daughter.

"Is that it?" asked the dwarf, and he stood up on the table. "Lovely-limbed. Yes, I'm sure she is."

"Sit down!" Thor told him irascibly.

"Still more?" Alvis taunted him.

"What about day's opposite? What are the names for night?"

"Ah!" said the dwarf. "Men and women and children say Night and the gods say Darkness but the most holy gods call it Hood. The giants say Lightness, the elves Sleep's Soothing and we dwarfs the Weaver of Dreams."

"What's the name of the seed sown by humans?"

"People say Barley, the Warrior Gods say Grain and the Green-and-Gold Gods say Growth. The giants call it Good-to-Eat, and the elves Drink Grist. Down in Hel it's called Slender Stem."

Thor reached out for a jug of ale, poured some into a horn and offered it to the dwarf. "This ale," he said, "the ale we all drink. What are its names?"

"Well, humans call it Ale," the dwarf replied. He stuck his pale nose into the ale Thor had given him, and then he sipped it. "You gods, you say Ale or Beer and the Green-and-Gold Gods say Foaming. Giants call it Shining Swill. Down in Hel the dead call it Mead."

"Mmm!" murmured Thor, and his voice sounded like the far-off growling of the sea. "It's true, Alvis, very true, I've never heard of anyone who knows as much as you about naming in the nine worlds – all the names my father taught me when I was as young as little Magni."

"What? No more questions?" Alvis mocked him.

Thor picked his teeth and swilled a mouthful of ale. "Such great wisdom, Alvis! Such age-old learning!"

"Thrud!" said Alvis, and his voice was hoarse and urgent.

Thor smiled and slowly nodded. "Alvis," he said. "Look, Alvis!"

The dwarf buried his face in his hands, and tried to hide from the shaft of sunlight piercing the hall and flooding along the tabletop.

He was too late, though.

"Your own sweet tongue has trapped you," gloated Thor.

And so it had. The rising Sun had seen Alvis and turned him into stone.

BALDER'S
▪DREAMS

The old may hang with the hides and have shrivelled skins but they often give good advice.

Balder's wife, Nanna, lay beside her husband.

At first she thought that if she kept very still, he would soon settle.

But no, he didn't.

Then she thought that if she were to rest a cool hand on his hot brow, his fevered breathing would ease, and he would grow calm.

Lying on her side in the half-light, Nanna gazed at the god she so loved – the god whom the giantess Skadi had wanted to marry, and all the other gods called the fairest, the most gentle of them all.

Balder mumbled.

He moaned.

And while sweet Nanna held her breath for fear that her very breathing would further disturb him, Balder began to wring his wrists, and lock his fingers into fists.

Then the god yelled. He flailed, he kicked, as if he were fighting off some enemy. Nanna threw her arms around him and called him back from whatever was tormenting him – "Balder! My Balder!" she cried – and she woke him.

Balder was unable to tell Nanna exactly what he had dreamed, only that he had been surrounded by dark shapes, writhing dark shapes closing in on him, intent on snuffing out the light of him.

Next morning, Balder told the council of gods and goddesses about his dreams, and no one was able to explain them.

Then Odin stood up. "I sacrificed one eye at the Well of Mimir," he called out. "I gave it not only for wisdom but the thirst for greater wisdom. I will saddle Sleipnir and ride down myself to the underworld. I will take my son Balder's dreams with me, and bring back their meanings."

▪ ◆ ▪

Down Odin rode, nine days and nine nights down and northward into

Niflheim, the realm of freezing mist and darkness.

In the cave at the entrance to Niflheim, the hell-hound called Garm heard Odin coming. Caked in blood, he began to howl, but he was unable to break loose from his chains. His time had not yet come.

One-eyed Allfather ignored Garm. He galloped on until he reached the hall of Loki's daughter, Hel.

There, by the eastern door, Odin dismounted. And while Sleipnir was still blowing out breath-balloons that froze and burst in front of them, Odin stepped into the vast gloomy hall and saw all the tables and benches were already laid, and decorated with shining gold rings, as if Hel were awaiting some great guest. Then Odin backed out and walked across to the earth-mound where a seeress – a wise woman – lay buried.

With his one fearsome eye, Odin stared at the grave. He stood utterly still and trained all of himself on the grave, and then began to murmur magic charms he had learned when he hung for nine nights on the great ash tree, Yggdrasill.

The spectre of a wise woman slowly began to rise from her earth-mound.

"Snow has drifted around my shoulders," she moaned. "Sheets of rain have drenched me. Dew has seeped into me. I have been dead for years, many years."

Odin did not take his eye off the seeress. Not for one moment.

"Who is the stranger who unearths me?"

"My name is Wanderer," Odin replied. "All the tables and benches in Hel's hall are strewn with gold rings. Whom are you expecting?"

The seeress groaned. "Balder," she moaned. "The shining mead in Hel's hall is being brewed to welcome Balder. Against my will I speak. I will say not one word more."

Not for a moment did Allfather

take his glittering eye off the seeress.

"Whatever I ask, you will answer me," he told her. "Who will steal the life of Odin's son?"

"His own brother," replied the seeress. "Hod will hurl the branch, and steal the life of Odin's son. Against my will I speak. I will say not one word more."

But still Odin held the seeress with his glittering eye. "Wise woman," he said, "who will take vengeance for Balder's death? Who will light the pyre for his murderer?"

"He has not been born," the seeress moaned. "He will be the son of Odin and the goddess Rind, and his name will be Vali. When he is only one day old, Vali will fight Hod. His hands will never have been washed and his hair never combed when he carries blind Hod to the pyre. Against my will I speak. I will say not one word more."

"Wise woman," said Odin, "you must answer whatever I ask. What are the names of all the grieving maidens who will weep salt, and shriek, and hurl their scarves sky-high?"

The seeress loomed in front of Allfather. She seemed to swirl around him, so that he was caught in her sickly gleam.

"You are not Wanderer," the wise woman slowly replied. "I know who you are: you're Odin the magician, as old as time."

Allfather blinked and lowered his gaze. Now that the seeress had recognized who he was, and named him, she had taken away his power; he could no longer oblige her to speak.

"Ride home, Odin," the wise woman gloated. "Ride back to Asgard and boast about our meeting. Never again will anyone raise me until Fenrir breaks loose from his chains, and the gods fight against giants and monsters, and the nine worlds burn to their foundations."

Odin could no longer restrain the wise woman. She began to ooze back into her earth-mound, and sank from sight.

But even after she had disappeared, the wise woman still shone and floated in front of Odin. Mournfully, Balder's father walked his horse to the deep root of the ash tree Yggdrasill — the one that burrows into Niflheim. There he watered Sleipnir and for a long while he watched the squirrel Ratatosk whisking up and down the peeling trunk, carrying insults from the dragon Nidhogg, lying at the foot of the tree, to the eagle on the topmost bough.

Above him and around him, the Guardian Tree listened and whispered. Nourished as it was by the three Norns who shape the course of each and every life, what was there it did not already know?

THE DEATH OF BALDER

Humans die, animals die,

but one thing never dies:

the name we leave behind us.

In Hel's hall ... shining mead to welcome him ... Balder ... Balder ... his own brother will steal his life...

Odin had found out the meaning of Balder's terrible dreams but not how to guard or save him.

This is what the gods and goddesses discussed as soon as they met in council. They resolved that no amount of effort should be spared to protect the best and most beautiful of them all, and they asked Frigg, Balder's mother and greatest of the goddesses, to travel through the nine worlds with her servant, the goddess Fulla, to secure an oath from each and every kind of peril that it would not harm Balder.

Fire swore an oath and Water swore an oath. Frigg persuaded Iron and Copper and Tin and every other kind of metal to swear oaths. Lightning swore an oath, each kind of stone swore an oath, trees and illnesses and animals and birds and poisonous plants and shrithing snakes, they all swore oaths.

"Nothing in the nine worlds will harm Balder," Frigg reassured Balder and the gods and goddesses when they all met again in the hall Gladsheim. "You can sleep in peace. We can all sleep in peace."

"We must put it to the test," said Odin. "Go on, Thor!"

Thor rubbed his thick head. "What?" he asked.

"Just tap Balder on the head with your hammer."

So that's what Thor did, and Iron kept its oath and withheld its strength. Balder wasn't even sure whether or not Mjollnir had touched the top of his head.

Although Odin still looked rather thoughtful, the other gods and goddesses laughed. They all praised Frigg for her powers of persuasion, and streamed out of the hall into the sunlight.

◆ ◆ ◆

Sometimes the gods drank together. Sometimes they listened while Bragi sang-and-said poems about their great adventures and feats, and made them laugh or weep at the strange ways of human beings. Sometimes the gods sang themselves, and sometimes they boasted. Sometimes they ran races on the Plain of Ida, they lifted weights, they wrestled. But now they had a new amusement – and that was to test and test again all the oaths that Frigg had secured, so as to be

sure that nothing in the nine worlds would ever harm Balder.

To begin with, the gods asked him to stand in the courtyard outside Gladsheim while they threw pebbles and little lumps of chalk at him, but soon they grew more daring and hurled jagged pieces of flint, and then they whacked Balder with wooden stakes and jabbed him with the points of jack-knives. Balder just smiled, and sometimes laughed, and the gods marvelled when none of their weapons were able to harm him.

Loki watched the gods, contemptuous of the way they were so easily amused. *They're like very young children*, he thought. *They've never grown up. No wonder I can outwit them again and again.*

Loki watched the way in which the three most beautiful goddesses of all, Idun and Freyja and Sif, fawned over Balder, and kept checking that he hadn't been injured. And it made the trickster's toes curl to see how Balder's mother, Frigg, sometimes presided over them all, clucking and smiling.

If they only knew about each other half of what I know about them, Loki thought. *Yes, almost all of them... Bragi the poet, he's pink-cheeked and girlish... Idun, she wrapped her arms around the man who murdered her brother... As for shameless Freyja, she sold her body to four dwarfs...*

Venom feeds off venom, and the more Loki watched the gods and goddesses, the more he loathed the whole lot of them.

His mind darkened. His saliva tasted bitter, his cheeks curdled, as if he'd been chewing a mouthful of sloes.

One morning Loki noticed that Frigg was missing from the daily council in Gladsheim, and then he had an idea. In the same copse where he'd once changed himself into a filly and frolicked with the stallion of the giant mason, he turned himself into an old woman and set off in search of Balder's mother.

The trickster walked across the Plain of Ida to the Water Halls, the buildings belonging to Balder's mother.

"Have you seen what the gods and goddesses are doing?" he asked her.

"What?" asked Frigg.

"Stoning someone. Someone with a white face ... shining fair hair..."

Frigg smiled.

"And they're trying to finish him off with knives and axes."

Frigg shook her head. "No, no, nothing will hurt my son, and he knows that. Each and every thing has sworn an oath that it will not harm him."

"Each and every thing?" repeated the old woman.

"So that we can all sleep in peace," Frigg told him.

"Each and every thing?" the old woman asked again. "Are you sure?"

"Well," said Frigg, waving her right hand, "everything except the mistletoe. The sprigs are so tender, the eyes so pale. It's the plant of peace. It wasn't worth bothering with."

"Is that so?" the old woman said.

And away she went. She hurried to a grove where mistletoe was growing out of the trunk of an oak, and changed herself back into Loki.

The trickster wrenched the mistletoe bush from the tree. He snapped off all the little sprigs until he was holding only the longest branch, and he sharpened one end of it.

Then Loki hurried back to Gladsheim, and there the gods and goddesses were once again amusing themselves by trying out new ways of harming Balder.

If only they knew, he thought... His eyes shone green and orange. *You, Freyr, you had to give away your sword to your own servant Skirnir so you could sleep with Gerd... You, Heimdall, you're nothing but a menial watchman. No better than a servant... You, Frigg, haven't you shared your bed with your husband's two brothers?... Yes, if you all knew half of what I know, you'd be tearing each other's throats out.*

Loki saw that Balder's blind brother,

Hod, was standing well to one side of all the other gods and goddesses, and he walked up and jabbed him in the ribs with the pointed end of the mistletoe branch.

"Hod!" he said. "My old friend. Why aren't you throwing things at your brother?"

"Why do you think?" asked Hod.

"Sometimes it's better not to see," Loki hissed.

"Sometimes," Hod replied, "it's better to have a choice."

Loki sighed.

"And even if I could see," added Hod, "I haven't got a weapon."

"Your brother's going to think that by standing apart and aloof, you're saying you're above him and all these tests, and games."

"No, he won't," said Hod.

"All the gods and goddesses are honouring Balder. They're checking that nothing whatsoever will harm him. You must do the same."

Hod was silent.

"I'll show you where he's standing," Loki whispered. "Then you can throw this little mistletoe twig at him."

Hod took the mistletoe and Loki guided his right arm.

The trickster bared his teeth and gave Balder a hideous smile. He guided Hod's right hand. He aimed the pointed twig at Balder and howled, and the twig pierced Balder and went right through him.

Balder fell to the ground, dead.

In Gladsheim, the Place of Joy, there was silence.

Not one sound.

All creation held its breath.

And when at last the gods turned to each other, stricken, still silent, they all suspected who had really caused the god's death. But they were unable to take vengeance there and then, because Gladsheim was holy ground, a sanctuary where no one could spill blood.

And no one understood better than his own all-seeing father, Odin, what the loss of Balder meant for them all. "Of all the things that have ever happened in the nine worlds," he said, "this is the most terrible."

Loki sneaked out of the hall, taking Hod with him, and the gods and goddesses sobbed.

They keened.

And after a while, Frigg called out, "Is there any god here who wishes to win all the love I can give him, and all the favours I can bestow on him? Who here will ride down to Niflheim and try to find Balder? Who will offer Hel a ransom if she allows my son to come home to Asgard?"

Frigg's own son Hermod took a step towards her. "I will," his voice rang out. "Hermod the Bold, that's what you call me, and that's what I am."

Servants at once left the hall and caught Odin's horse Sleipnir. They saddled and reined him and brought him to Allfather.

There was no need for more words. Sometimes even words fail.

Odin gave the reins to his son, then Hermod embraced Frigg and mounted Sleipnir. He looked around him at the moon-faces of all the gods and goddesses. Then he raised his right hand and galloped away.

■ ■ ■

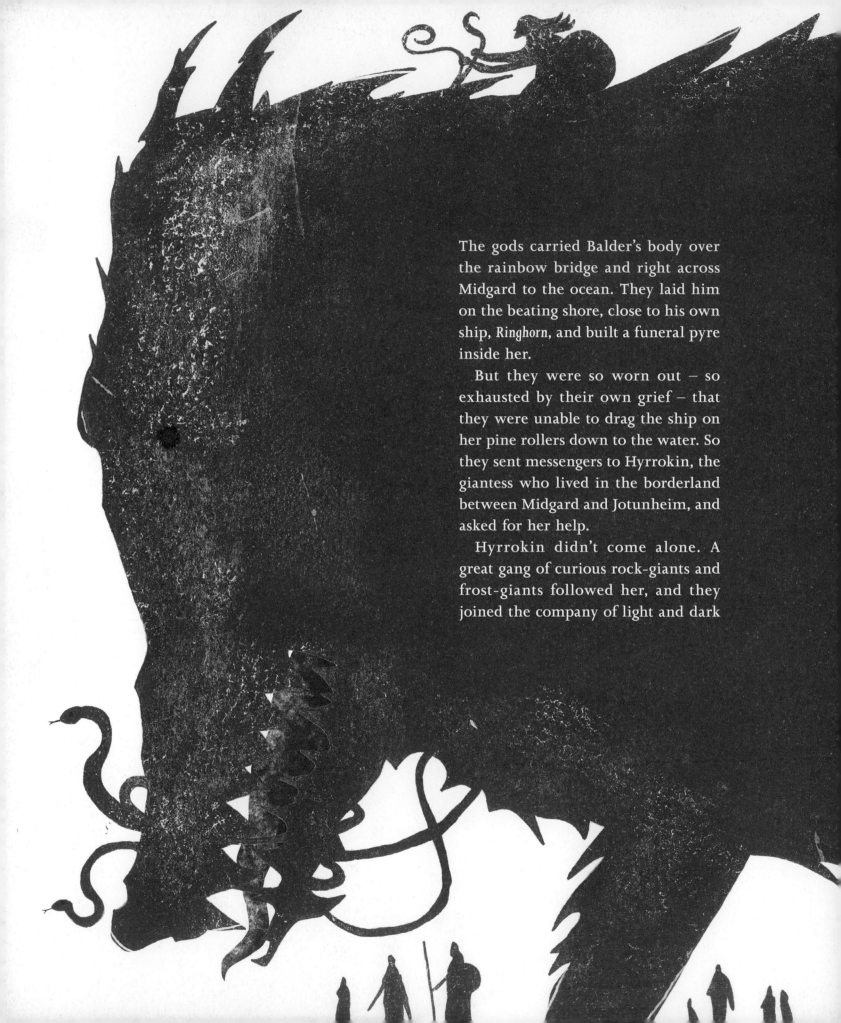

The gods carried Balder's body over the rainbow bridge and right across Midgard to the ocean. They laid him on the beating shore, close to his own ship, *Ringhorn*, and built a funeral pyre inside her.

But they were so worn out – so exhausted by their own grief – that they were unable to drag the ship on her pine rollers down to the water. So they sent messengers to Hyrrokin, the giantess who lived in the borderland between Midgard and Jotunheim, and asked for her help.

Hyrrokin didn't come alone. A great gang of curious rock-giants and frost-giants followed her, and they joined the company of light and dark elves and dwarfs and men and women and children who had all heard of Balder's death and were gathering on the foreshore.

Hyrrokin was huge and she was riding a wolf half as large as Fenrir, with vipers for reins.

Odin didn't like the look of the wolf at all, so he instructed four fighting men wearing nothing but bear-skins to keep a very careful eye on him. But even when the men had seized his viper-reins, they were unable to handle him. The wolf snarled and foamed and dragged them this way and that, so the men used the clubs of their bare fists. They beat him down onto the sand.

Hyrrokin stumped right round graceful *Ringhorn*. Then she spat on her palms and grabbed the curved prow. She dug in her heels as deeply as she could and jerked the ship so fiercely that *Ringhorn* raced forward, screaming. The pine rollers burst into flames. The whole world trembled.

"How dare you?" shouted Thor. "How dare you show such disrespect?"

Odin put a hand on Thor's right shoulder.

"I'll crack her skull!" cried the thunder god.

"No," said Odin. "We asked Hyrrokin for help. We can't attack a guest."

Then a group of gods lifted Balder and stepped out through the shallows, and carefully laid his body on the pyre.

Nanna's heart pounded so loudly she could hear neither the sobbing all around her nor the mewing of the gulls, the little dashes of the waves.

Her pain was too great. Nanna's heart broke, and she collapsed and died there on the strand. The grieving goddesses and gods carried her body out to *Ringhorn* and when they had laid her beside her husband Balder, they lit the pyre.

After this, one of his servants rode Balder's horse along the foreshore until he had worked up a fine sweat. Still wearing his saddle and harness, the horse was walked towards the stern, and there the servant plunged a dagger into his throat. Several men at once helped to hack his steaming body into huge pieces, and threw them onto the smoking pyre.

Thor raised Mjollnir. With the old words that had been used for as long as anyone could remember, he consecrated the pyre, and everyone there bowed their heads: Freyr in his chariot drawn by the silver-gold boar, Gullinbursti; his sister Freyja in her chariot drawn by cats; Heimdall on his stallion, Gold Tuft; gods and goddesses, men and women and children, they all attended, everyone except for a dwarf called Lit who had lost any interest in the ceremony.

Lit came scampering along the foreshore right in front of Thor, and the thunder god stuck out a foot and tripped him. The dwarf fell flat on his face and, before he could pick himself up, Thor kicked him straight onto the pyre, and Lit was burned to death.

Odin splashed out through the shallows. He hauled himself over *Ringhorn*'s gunwales and slipped over Balder's wrist his own gold armband Draupnir that dripped eight rings of the same weight and value every ninth night.

Then Allfather bowed his head and put his mouth to Balder's ear. No one could hear what words he whispered; not then, and not since.

So at last, *Ringhorn*'s anchor was pulled up and her painter thrown into the stern. The salt waves lifted her, cradled her, lifted her. Away she drifted while a plume of smoke rose from the pyre, and a light wind shredded it.

On the foreshore, everyone watched. Gods and friends of the gods, foes of the gods, the merely curious, they all knew that unless Hel would agree to let Balder come home to Asgard, his death – the death of the handsome god who cherished and protected whatever was beautiful, and patient, and innocent in the nine worlds – must bring closer their own death-day.

▪ ▰ ▪

Hermod and Sleipnir nosed their way through the dark. For nine nights they rode through deep valleys until they reached the river Gjoll and the bridge over it, thatched with straw of pure gold.

The warden of the bridge, a maiden called Modgud, stepped out in front of them and she stared at Hermod.

"Yesterday," she said, "five groups of dead men rode over this bridge but you and your horse are making more noise than they all did together. Anyhow, you don't look like a dead man."

"I'm not," said Hermod.

"Who are you, then?" asked Modgud. "And why are you riding down to Hel?"

"I am Hermod, and I'm searching for my brother."

"Brother?"

"Balder. Have you seen him? Did he come this way?"

Modgud lowered her grey eyes. "He crossed this bridge – the way of the dead to Hel."

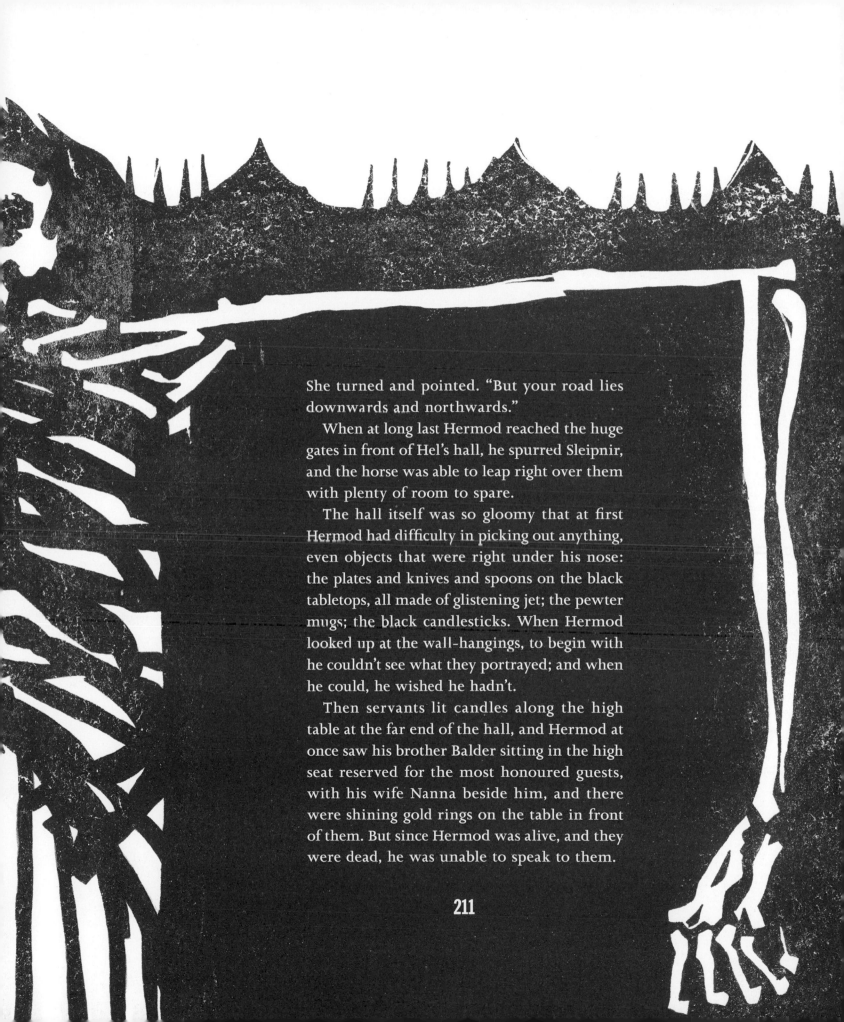

She turned and pointed. "But your road lies downwards and northwards."

When at long last Hermod reached the huge gates in front of Hel's hall, he spurred Sleipnir, and the horse was able to leap right over them with plenty of room to spare.

The hall itself was so gloomy that at first Hermod had difficulty in picking out anything, even objects that were right under his nose: the plates and knives and spoons on the black tabletops, all made of glistening jet; the pewter mugs; the black candlesticks. When Hermod looked up at the wall-hangings, to begin with he couldn't see what they portrayed; and when he could, he wished he hadn't.

Then servants lit candles along the high table at the far end of the hall, and Hermod at once saw his brother Balder sitting in the high seat reserved for the most honoured guests, with his wife Nanna beside him, and there were shining gold rings on the table in front of them. But since Hermod was alive, and they were dead, he was unable to speak to them.

211

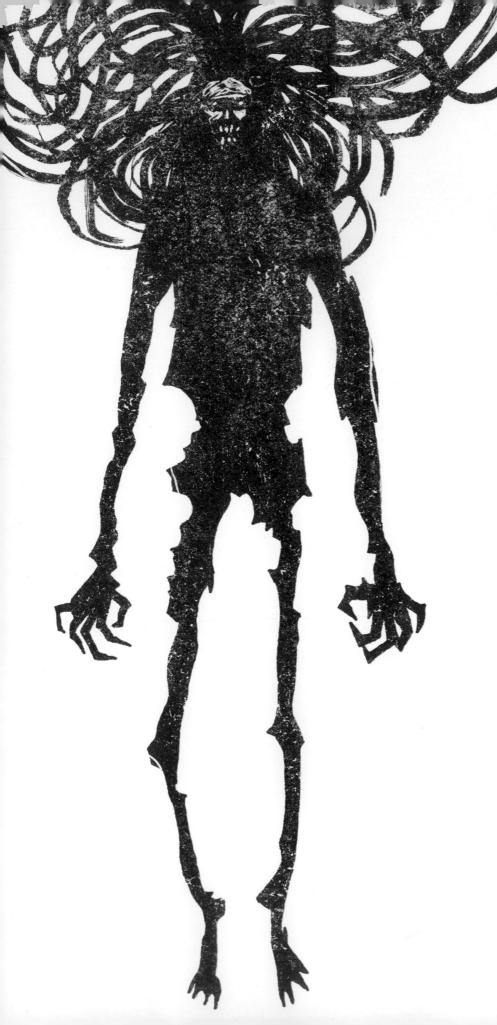

Early the next morning, Hermod approached Hel, Loki's daughter, and sat down in front of her. Her appearance hadn't improved since Allfather had thrown her out of Asgard, and the top half of her body was that of a living old woman while the bottom half was a blackened corpse. Her skin was papery and her flaring eyes had somehow retreated into her head. She didn't smile, and perhaps she never had.

Hermod explained to Hel how all the gods and goddesses in Asgard were stricken with grief, and how their tears were not only for themselves but for everyone and everything in the nine worlds.

"Will you allow Balder to ride home with me?" he asked.

Hermod had to wait rather a long time for Hel to reply, and when she did so, it was in a high, somehow pinched voice.

"Allfather banished me from Asgard. What was good enough for me is good enough for Balder."

"In the name of all creation," Hermod pleaded, "allow my brother to ride home with me."

"Balder is dead," Hel replied. "This is his home." She

moistened her scaly lips. "Is Balder really loved as much as people say?" she asked. "We must put it to the test." She gave Hermod a grim look. "If everything in the nine worlds, dead and alive, will weep for him, as once they swore never to harm him, he can return to Asgard. But if anyone or anything will not weep, he must remain here with me."

Hermod stood up and Balder and Nanna silently led him out of the hall. In the courtyard, Balder took off Draupnir — the gold armband Odin had slipped over his wrist on his funeral pyre — and gestured that Hermod should give it back to him. And Nanna gave Hermod a spread of linen sufficient to make a headdress, and a golden finger-ring, and gestured that he should give them to Frigg and her servant Fulla.

Hermod mounted Sleipnir. He gazed at Balder and Nanna. So lovingly. So sadly. And with a heavy heart he rode away.

■ ▰ ■

As soon as Hermod had returned to Asgard and repeated Hel's condition, word for word, the gods sent out messengers into each of the worlds, asking everyone and everything to weep Balder out of Hel.

And that's what they did. Fire wept and Water wept. Iron and Copper and Tin and every other kind of metal wept. Lightning wept and each kind of stone

wept. Trees and illnesses and animals and birds and poisonous plants and shrithing snakes, they all wept — just as things weep when frost thaws and they begin to grow warm.

Well pleased with their work, the messengers were on their way back to the rainbow bridge when they saw a cave. And when they entered the cave, they found a giantess sitting on a large rock. She told them her name was Thokk.

"Will you weep for Balder?" they asked her. "Weep for Balder and weep him out of Hel?"

Thokk's eyes glistened. She tightened her twisted mouth as if she were almost smiling.

"The tears Thokk will weep are dry tears," she rasped.

"No!" cried one messenger.

"But—" began another.

"Alive or dead, what use has Balder ever been to me?" the giantess demanded. "Let Hel hold what she has."

Mournful and full of foreboding the messengers crossed Bifrost. They trooped to the hall Gladsheim and reported how everyone and everything had wept for Balder, everyone except for the giantess sitting in the cave.

In their heads and their hearts, the grieving gods and goddesses all knew that Thokk was Loki. They knew that Balder would have to remain in Hel and would never be able to return to Asgard.

VENGEANCE

**Expect those you've
wronged to try to
settle the score.**

Loki was elated. He was on fire at having guided blind Hod's hand and caused Balder's death, and he choked with laughter at having prevented him from being wept out of Hel.

But he knew the cost as well. He knew the gods and goddesses were appalled, because Balder was the best of them and his death foretold their own, and Loki knew they would go to the ends of the nine worlds to take vengeance on him. He knew that never again would he walk across the sweet meadows of Asgard, and he was terrified. His blood seethed, his blood froze.

Somehow or other Loki sneaked over Bifrost and escaped.

"I would have blown my shrieking horn," Heimdall said, "but I didn't see him. I saw nothing. Not even a shadow."

Loki didn't know where to hide. Yes, he did. No, he didn't.

As he made off across Midgard, to begin with he kept thinking he was being followed. When he saw a falcon hovering, he was sure it was about to drop on him and he put his arms over the top of his head. When he hurried through a gloomy wood, half the trees turned into scowling giants.

But the day lengthened, and the Sun shone, and for a while Loki almost escaped himself.

Before dusk, he walked well up into the mountains, far beyond herdsmen and their cattle and sheep, higher even than skipping goats, and reached a kind of rocky tabletop, where the land fell away on all four sides.

This is where Loki built a low-slung stone room out of rocks and rubble, and it had four doors so that he could see out of it in all four directions.

Even so, his own feelings and fears kept getting the better of him.

One moment he was gleeful, the next shuddering. He was even nervous of a bank of dark clouds – they seemed to be closing in on him, and threatening to snuff him out.

So as to be more safe in the bright daylight, Loki turned himself into a salmon. He hid in the furious water at the bottom of Franang's Falls.

But at night, in his stone room, he sat beside his fire and kept working out the ways in which the gods could still catch him, and how to escape them. One evening he twisted lengths of linen twine, and laid them across his lap. Then he braided a very fine mesh – a mesh that could catch fish and tricksters and demons – and that's how the best nets have been made ever since.

▪ ▪ ▪

From his high seat, Hlidskjalf, Odin searched the nine worlds for Loki, and with his one, burning eye, he found him. At once Allfather summoned all the gods and goddesses to his hall, Valaskjalf, and dispatched Thor and Tyr and Njord to capture Loki.

Loki saw them coming. He threw his twine net into the fire, and hurried out of his stone house. He ran down to Franang's Falls, changed himself into a salmon and leaped into the whirling pool.

At first, the gods could see nothing inside the sparse, gloomy stone room that gave them the least idea where Loki had gone. But then Njord, god of seafarers, detected a pattern in the fireplace – a criss-crossing of white ash and grey ash.

"This was a kind of net," he told the others.

"More finely meshed than Ran's net," said Tyr. "The one she uses to drown men and women."

"And finer than the one fishermen use to catch fish," Njord said. "Let us make a net, like this."

When the gods had woven the net, they scrambled down to Franang's Falls. Then Thor asked his companions to hold one end of the net while he splashed across the pool, grasping the other end. But Loki saw the gods lowering their drag-net and sculled down the river in front of it, and then he nestled between two boulders while the net brushed his back.

All the same, Njord and Tyr were quite sure they had seen something in the sluicing water, something as dark as a shadow, quivering and agile. So the three gods decided to drag the river again, and this time they weighted their net with stones.

There was nowhere Loki could hide now, so when the river began to pan out into shallows before plunging over a cliff into the sea, the trickster arched his back, rainbowed his whole body,

leaped back over the net and swam back up to the waterfall.

"We must drag the river once more," Thor said, "and then we'll have him. You two walk on either side, and I'll wade down the middle."

This is what they did, and as they neared the shallows again, Loki could see his choice: either to squirm and wallop over the shallows and try to reach the cliff-edge before the gods reached him, or to leap back over the drag-net for a second time.

The salmon turned and rushed towards the net, and he sprang right over it, silver and strong and most beautiful.

Thor reached out. He clutched him. Bucking and writhing and twisting, the salmon started to slip through the god's fingers, but Thor squeezed and held him tight. The trickster was unable to escape – and that's why salmon taper towards their tails.

■ ◢ ■

While Thor and Tyr escorted Loki to a cave, Njord returned to Asgard to seek the help of more gods and goddesses as well as his own wife Skadi, and they divided into three groups.

The first group headed for the cave, and there they propped up three flat white stones on their rims – they looked like huge plates or saucers – and bored a hole through each of them.

Another group searched for Loki's faithful wife, Sigyn, and told her they had captured him and where she could find him.

The third group hunted down two of Loki's sons, Vali and Narfi. They changed Vali into a wolf, and the first thing he did was round on his younger brother and tear him to pieces. Then Vali galloped away and down into the underworld, howling.

All the gods then returned to the cave, and there they laid out Loki, face up over the three stones – one beneath his scrawny shoulders, one below his hips, one behind his knees.

Then they bound him with the gut of his own son, Narfi. And the moment Loki was bound, each of these bonds turned into iron.

Sigyn keened for her husband. She keened for her two sons.

True, Loki the trickster had once made Skadi smile by unrolling himself and then leaping onto her shoulder, but the snow-shoe giantess had never forgotten how he caused her own father Thiazi's death by luring him back to Asgard. She reached right up to the roof of the cave, and there she fastened a poisonous snake so that its venom would drip straight onto Loki's face.

Loki screwed up his eyes. He didn't flinch. He said not a single word. He gave the gods no satisfaction whatsoever by showing them his feelings – his ghastly suffering, his hatred and self-hatred, his volcanic fury, his passion to take revenge. After a long while, the gods all turned away from him and slowly walked back to Asgard.

All except loyal Sigyn. Well knowing her husband's wickedness, she sobbed for him. She sobbed bitter tears for her sons. Helpless, she wept at the cruelty of the gods. She wept for each suffering woman in the world.

Holding a large wooden bowl to catch the drops of venom, Sigyn sat beside Loki. That's where she still sits…

Each drop echoes as it splashes into the bowl. That's the only sound in the gloomy cave: that and the soft sound of Sigyn's and Loki's breathing.

But slowly the basin fills, and when it's brimming, Sigyn has to stand up and tip away all the poison into a bubbling pit at the mouth of the cave.

The snake doesn't wait. It goes on dripping venom onto Loki's face, and he cannot escape. He writhes, he shudders and shakes. And that's what everyone calls an earthquake.

There, in the cave, Loki lies bound with the gut of his own son. That's how things are and how they will be until the gods fight against the giants and monsters, and the nine worlds burn, and Midgard and Asgard sink into the sea.

THE LAST BATTLE

No one can deny Fate. Her gifts are unearned

and her punishments undeserved.

Gylfi, King of Sweden, grew old.

After he had crossed the rainbow bridge for the first time, disguised as a tramp called Gangleri, and talked in Valhalla to the three mysterious wise kings, High One and Just-as-High and Third, he sent out messengers through Midgard searching for stories about the gods and goddesses, and he asked his scribes to write them down so that people would not forget them.

But now and then the king remembered how the three kings had lowered their eyes when they spoke of Balder, and told him that Odin would soon need all the dead warriors he had seen in Valhalla; and he remembered that they hadn't replied to his question: "Must whatever begins also end?"

So, when he was an old man, Gylfi decided to return to Valhalla, to seek out the three kings, and to ask them to tell him not only what had happened in the nine worlds but what would happen.

The old king disguised himself again as Gangleri. Slowly he trudged over Bifrost, he greeted Heimdall, and shuffled along the wide path until he reached the huge hall, Valhalla, with its roof of overlapping gold shields.

The three kings, High One, Just-as-High and Third, saw Gangleri coming. They combed their beards, and settled into their three high seats, one above the other.

"You again," said High One, and he nodded.

"We've been expecting you," Just-as-High told him.

"Step forward, please," said Third.

"I want to know," Gangleri told them, "not only what has happened in the nine worlds but what will happen."

"And happen soon," High One said in a gloomy voice.

"Must whatever begins also end?" asked Gangleri.

For a while the three kings sat silent, as if the very thought of what was to happen had locked their words inside them.

"Not in your lifetime," High One said, "and not in the lifetimes of your children or grandchildren, but all too soon."

"In Midgard, the world of human beings," began Third, "families will round on each other and fall apart. Brothers will not laugh but argue, and then they'll draw knives and kill each other. Men will bed each other's wives. Most people will put gold and their own gain before law and order. For three years, there will be feuds and skirmishes all over Midgard, and after that pitched battles."

Gangleri lowered his head.

"And then," Just-as-High went on, "there'll be three winters such as no one has ever known or even heard of, unbroken winters with no spring, no summer, no autumn between them. Bands of snow; ice-floes; whirlwinds; biting cold."

"Axe-age and sword-age, storm-age, wolf-age," said High One. "Nothing but hatred and revenge instead of loyalty and friendship."

Gangleri's eyes misted with tears. He hung his grey head.

"This is just the beginning of the end," High One went on. "Did we ever tell you how the two wolves Skoll and Hati chase the Sun? Skoll will catch the Sun and swallow her. And Hati will catch the Moon and spit his blood all over the sky, and swallow him. Then all the thousands of stars will be snuffed out."

Gangleri shuddered. "Do not tell me, but tell me," he intoned in a low voice. "I must know."

"Gangleri," said Just-as-High, "you may well shudder. The ground beneath your feet, the earth itself will shudder. Great trees will be uprooted. The sides of whole mountains will come crashing down – cascades of rocks and gravel."

"Storms will whip sand and dust into the eyes of each and every living thing," Third went on. "Brown-eyed foxes and blue-eyed horses will scream in terror. More? Will you hear more?"

Gangleri jerked his head.

"Thick ropes made of hairy sisal," Third told him, "and chains of wrought iron, they'll snap or be ripped apart. Even magic spells will lose their power. That's when the wolf Fenrir will burst Gleipnir, the magic ribbon made by the dwarfs. Ah! You've heard that story…"

Gangleri nodded.

"Yes, he'll crush the sword that Tyr jammed into his mouth and lope across the Plain of Ida with his lower jaw pressed against the earth and his upper jaw against the sky – and if there were more room, his mouth would gape even wider. Fenrir will snort flames and his eyes will be blazing."

"Meanwhile," said High One, "the Midgard Serpent, Jormungand, will start to writhe as he comes ashore. Huge waves will lash all the cliffs and coves and bights and beaches of Midgard."

"Many men and women will drown," said Just-as-High. "Many children will drown."

"Ghastly sea-eagles will tear dead bodies with their beaks," High One added, and Gangleri could hear his anger. "Some animals, some humans

know only how to help themselves."

"The giants are building a huge ship out of dead men's fingernails," Third went on, "and she will break her moorings."

Gangleri shook his poor head.

"So I'm warning you: when you hear someone has died, make sure his nails are properly cut. Otherwise that death-ship, and its giant helmsman Hrym, will be ready to sail all the sooner."

"Gangleri," said Just-as-High, "after

Jormungand has come ashore, the dark sky will be torn in two, and the black giant Surt who guards Muspell, the realm of fire, will come charging through it. He'll be brandishing his sword that glares even more brightly than the Sun. He and his followers will crack and break Bifrost when they ride across it."

"Yes," said Third. "They'll head for the huge plain called Vigrid on the far side of Asgard. It's more than three hundred miles from one side to the other. Fenrir and his brother Jormungand will be on their way there too, and all the frost-giants will hurry to meet them. Ah, and Loki too. His ghastly bonds will burst because the magic that binds him will have lost its power. He'll escape from the cave and be waiting on the plain with his daughter Hel, risen from the underworld and leading her huge army of dead murderers and liars and thieves."

"This is when Heimdall will blow a great blast on his horn," Just-as-High told Gangleri. "He'll startle all the sleeping gods, and when they've met beside trembling Yggdrasill, Odin will gallop on his own to the Well of Mimir, where he gave his eye in search of further wisdom…"

For a long while, though it seemed so short to Gangleri, there was silence in Valhalla. The fighting men, the men playing chess, the servants – they were all listening to the three wise kings.

"All the gods will arm themselves," High One said in a calm voice. "All the dead warriors, fighting here in Valhalla and playing games and feasting each night, they will arm themselves, and surge towards the plain. Odin, our Allfather, will lead us."

"His glorious gold helmet," Just-as-High proclaimed, "will be decorated with great happenings."

"How the giant mason built the wall of Asgard for the gods," said Third. "How the dwarfs Brokk and Eitri forged Thor's hammer, Mjollnir. How Idun gives apples each day to the gods. How Otter's skin was covered with gold."

"Yes," said Gangleri. "With the red gold Loki won from the dwarf Andvari. Why has the trickster turned against you? Why did he bring about the death of Balder?"

"Once upon a time Loki chose to help us," High One replied, "and there have been many times when we forced him to save us. But what was good in him has been eaten by what's evil. Now … now he chooses to destroy us."

"Odin will be wearing a clinking coat of mail," Just-as-High said, "and it will spark and glitter in the light from Surt's sword. He'll be riding Sleipnir, and carrying his spear Gungnir. He'll make straight for the wolf Fenrir."

"Thor will be right beside him," added Third, "but he won't be able to help because the Midgard Serpent will be spitting poison at him."

"Freyr will battle with the black giant Surt," said Just-as-High, "but in the end Surt will fell him. Do you know why? Because Freyr gave away his own sword to his servant Skirnir as a reward."

Gangleri frowned and looked puzzled.

"Do you remember when Skirnir went down to the frost-giants and coaxed…"

"Threatened," High One corrected him.

"When Skirnir threatened beautiful Gerd," Just-as-High said, "until she swore to give herself to Freyr?"

"Ah, yes!" said Gangleri. "Yes, I remember."

"Like Fenrir and like Loki too," added Third, "the hell-hound, Garm, chained at the mouth of the underworld, will break free. He'll leap down from his cliff-cave, and bound up to the Plain of Vigrid. He and one-handed Tyr will fight and kill each other."

"As for Loki," said High One, "the sly one, the trickster, the shape-changer…"

Gangleri's eyes widened.

"Heimdall will wrestle with him, and each will strangle the other."

All three rulers lowered their eyes. Their shoulders drooped. As if they could scarcely believe their own words, or believe the nine worlds would be plunged into such conflict and chaos.

"And Thor?" asked Gangleri slowly. "And the serpent's poison?"

"Jormungand is so terrible," High One replied, "that the only god who can take him on and hope to kill him is Thor. And that's what he'll do. He'll kill the Midgard Serpent with his hammer Mjollnir, but Jormungand will blow a storm of poison at his face. Thor will only be able to stagger nine steps back before he falls dead himself."

229

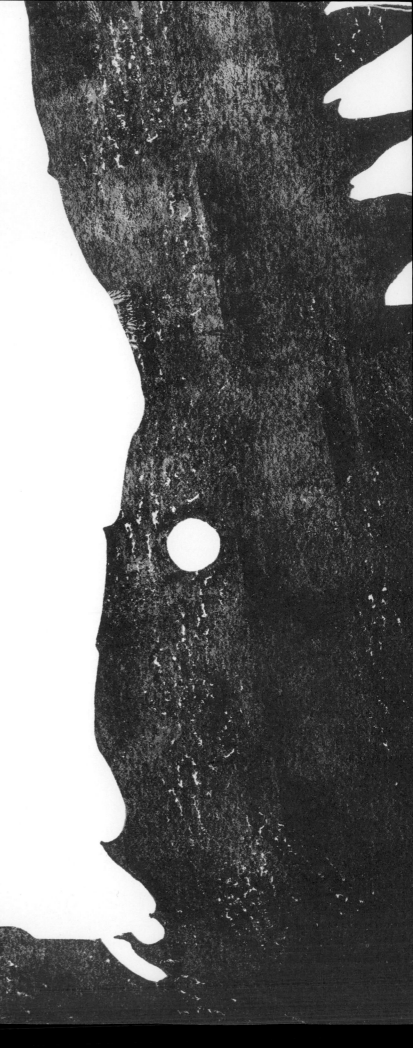

Gangleri closed his eyes.

"As for Odin," High One intoned in a low voice, and he shuddered. "As for Odin, his fight with Fenrir won't last long. The wolf will swallow him."

Gangleri gasped.

"Yes," said High One. "That's how Allfather himself, the Terrible One, the one-eyed god, the Father of Battle, the god with one hundred names, must die. But listen, Gangleri! Vidar, the son of Odin, will stride forward and put one foot on Fenrir's lower jaw."

Gangleri shook his head.

"Haven't you heard about the shoe he'll be wearing? He's been working at it since the beginning of time so as to be ready for this moment. It's made of all the little leather strips people pare from the heels and toes when they're making new shoes. If you want to help the gods, you must never throw them away or burn them. Vidar needs them for his shoe."

Gangleri nodded.

"Vidar," said High One, "will grab the wolf's upper jaw with one gloved hand, and he'll rip his jaws apart. That will be the end of Fenrir."

For a while the three kings sat in silence, and Gangleri realized he was panting.

"Will you hear more?" asked Just-as-High.

Third shook his head. "No one from Middle Earth has heard half as much."

"Surt will fling waves of fire north and south and east and west," High One told Gangleri. "The flames will lick heaven itself."

"So will we all burn to death?" Gangleri asked. "Men and women and children and even babies?"

"All human beings will," High One replied, "and so will all the gods."

"But I have heard," said Gangleri, scratching his head, "that when they die, people will still go on living."

High One nodded quite kindly. "Some huge halls will escape the flames," he

explained, "and in those halls the dead will go on living. Some will be for people who have lived good lives, some for people who have lived bad ones."

"There'll be a hall in the Dark Mountains," said Third, "and its roof and walls will be made of red gold."

"A home for good men and women," said Gangleri.

"One of many," said Third. "But there'll be a huge hall with walls made of snakes, woven together like wattle. You can imagine what kind of people will be wading around there."

"And beyond the halls," Gangleri asked, "will there be nothing? Will there just be emptiness, as it was in the beginning?"

"Gangleri," said High One, and he raised both his arms. "This will be the time, after our time ends, when the Mother Earth of Midgard and Asgard will rise again out of the heaving sea."

"Oh!" cried Gangleri, and he clapped his right hand over his mouth.

"Green – so green, so beautiful. Then fields of corn, fields that were never sown, will grow and ripen, silver and gold."

"But you said the wolf Skoll would catch the Sun and swallow her, and the world would wallow in darkness."

"Before she dies," Third explained, "the Sun will give birth to a daughter just as lovely as she is. And she'll follow the same sky-path as her mother."

"Will none of the gods survive?" Gangleri asked.

"Vidar and Vali, the sons of Odin, will be unscathed," Just-as-High replied. "And Thor's two sons, Modi and Magni, will escape unharmed, and they will inherit their father's hammer, Mjollnir. The four of them will live on the Plain of Ida, the meadows lying all around us. Balder and his brother Hod will journey up from Hel and join them here."

"I can see them now," said Third, "sitting there, sometimes keeping their thoughts to themselves, sometimes gently talking, remembering everything they held dear, remembering everything that happened in times past." He took a deep breath and slowly, very slowly, let it all out again. His eyelids trembled.

"They'll find the golden chessmen once owned by the gods," said Just-as-High, "lying on their sides in the waving grass."

"But in Midgard?" said Gangleri very quietly, as if he were talking to himself, "no men, you say … no women … no children?"

All three kings stood up in their seats, and High One spoke. "While Surt's fire rages, and the world dissolves to ashes and settles into dust, a man and a woman will hide in the heart of the World Tree, the Guardian Tree. Their names will be Life and Life-to-Be. For their food and drink, they'll sip the dew that each morning shines on the branches of Yggdrasill. They will have children, and their children will have children."

High One spread his arms as wide as the world.

He took a deep breath, the breath of life itself. "Now, Gangleri," he said, "if you've any more to ask, even a single question, I don't know who could answer it. I've never heard of anyone who could tell more about our worlds and their story."

Gangleri, tramp and king, closed his eyes and nodded.

"Tell these stories yourself," said the three kings, "and for as long as our worlds last, people will retell them. Make what use of them you can."

GLOSSARY

adder: a poisonous snake with zig-zag markings

Aegir: the god of the ocean, responsible for brewing the gods' ale, husband of Ran

Andvari: a dwarf who gives Loki the gold he needs to pay Otter's ransom

Angrboda: a giantess and the mother of three of Loki's children: Jormungand, Hel and Fenrir

anvil: a heavy metal block used by a blacksmith to hammer hot metal into a shape

Asgard: the top level of the Norse cosmos, home to the gods and goddesses

auger: a sharp tool used to make a hole

auroch: a wild ox

bait: the food put on a hook or a trap to attract fish or animals

Baugi: a giant, Suttung's brother

bellows: a device that blows air onto a fire to make it burn

Bifrost: the three-strand rainbow bridge that connects Asgard and Midgard

Bilskirnir: Thor's hall

bolster: a long, thick pillow used under other pillows

bow: the front part of a boat

Bragi: the god of poetry

bulrush: a tall reed-like water plant

capstone: the top finishing stone in a wall

cauldron: a very large metal pot

clay: a type of soil that can be mixed with water to create a material used to make pots or bricks

colt: a young male horse

coping: the stones on the top of a wall

copse: a group of trees

coulter: the sharp part of a plough that cuts into the soil

cupbearer: the person responsible for serving drinks at feasts

draughts: a board game

Draupnir: a magical arm-ring that will create new gold rings, made for Odin by the dwarfs Brokk and Eitri

duel: an arranged fight between two people to settle a dispute or point of honour

Eir: the goddess of healing

Elivagar: the river between Midgard and Jotunheim

Fafnir: the son of Hreidmar, brother of Otter

falcon: a bird of prey

fell: a hill or small mountain

Fenrir: a massive wolf, one of Loki and Angrboda's children

flay: to strip the skin from the body

flint: a hard rock, usually steely grey

forge: a place where metal is heated so that it can be shaped

frost-giants: the giants who live in the snow

Fulla: Frigg's servant

galumphing: a heavy, bounding movement

Garm: the hound who stands outside Niflheim, the world of the dead

gat-toothed: gap-toothed

gauntlet: a protective glove that covers the wrist

gauze: a thin see-through fabric

Gefion: a goddess, tricks the King of Sweden

Gilling: a giant drowned by the dwarfs Fjalar and Galar

Gladsheim: a great hall where the gods meet, known as the Place of Joy; a sacred place where no blood could be spilt

Gleipnir: the ribbon made by dwarfs to bind the wolf Fenrir

goblet: a drinking cup

Golden Mane: Hrungnir's horse

Green-and-Gold Gods: a group of gods, sometimes called the Vanir, associated with growth and harvest, including Freyr, Freyja and Njord

Grid: a giantess, mother of Vidar, helps Thor

Groa: a wise woman who knows charms and spells, wife of Aurvandil the brave

Gullinbursti: a silver boar with shining golden bristles, made for Freyr by the dwarfs Brokk and Eitri

Gungnir: a magical spear that will never miss its mark, made for Odin by the dwarfs Son One and Son Two

Gunnlod: a giantess, daughter of the giant Suttung

gunwale: the upper edge on a boat's side

Gylfi: the King of Sweden, disguises himself as a tramp called Gangleri

Gymir: a frost-giant, father of Gerd

hall: a large single-room building, used for gatherings, drinking and feasting

haunch: the leg and loin of an animal

hawk: to clear the throat noisily

hearth: the floor and area around a fireplace

Hel: one of Loki and Angrboda's children, half living woman and half corpse, lives in the realm of the dead in Niflheim, which is also known by her name

Hermod: a god, son of Odin and Frigg

Hlidskjalf: Odin's high seat

Hlora: the mother of Tyr

Hnitbjorg: the mountain where Suttung and Gunnlod live

Hod: a blind god, who is tricked by Loki into killing his brother Balder

Honir: a long-legged indecisive god

horn: a drinking container carved from an animal's horn

Hreidmar: a farmer and a magician, father of Otter, Fafnir and Regin

Hrungnir: the strongest of all the giants, has a stone heart

Hymir: a giant, married to Hlora, owner of a huge cauldron

Hyrrokin: giantess who helps at Balder's funeral

jack-knife: a knife with a folding blade

jet: a hard black stone

Jormungand: one of Loki and Angrboda's children, a serpent so large he can circle Midgard and bite his own tail, also known as the Midgard Serpent

Jotunheim: the realm of the giants in Midgard

keen: to mourn in a loud wailing voice

keg: a small barrel

kindling: the dry material used to start a fire

Kvasir: a wise half-man half-god, made from the spit of all the gods

lance: a long spear-like weapon

light elves: magical, beautiful creatures

lintel: the beam above a door

237

longhouse: single storey farmhouse, often with a roof made of turf

loom: a machine used by weavers to make fabric

Magni: Thor's young son with the giantess Iron Cutlass

mare: a female horse

marl: a mixture of clay and crushed limestone

mason: a builder who works with bricks or stone

mastiff: a large, powerful dog

mead: an alcoholic drink made from honey and water

mica: tiny glittering minerals found in granite rock

Midgard: the middle level of the Norse cosmos, home to humans, giants and dwarfs

millstone: a heavy stone used for grinding grain

mistletoe: an evergreen shrub that grows on other trees such as the apple tree and the oak, has white berries

Mjollnir: Thor's unbreakable hammer, made for him by the dwarfs Brokk and Eitri

Modgud: the maiden who guards the bridge over the river Gjoll

Modi: Thor's son

Muspell: the realm of fire

Nanna: Balder's wife

Narfi: Loki's son, killed by his brother Vali

Nidhogg: the dragon at the foot of Yggdrasill

Niflheim: the bottom level of the Norse cosmos, home to the dead

Noatun: Njord's hall

Norns: the three goddesses called Fate, Being and Necessity, who decide the destiny of every human

oath: a solemn and formal promise

ox: a large cow-like animal used for ploughing or pulling loads

painter: the rope used to tie up a boat

pitcher: a jug

Plain of Ida: a vast central space in Asgard

Plain of Vigrid: a huge open space in Asgard, site of the final battle between gods and man, giants and monsters

pottage: a thick soup

precipice: a steep cliff

prow: the very front part of a boat

quartz: a type of rock

Ragnarok: the final battle involving all creation

Ran: a goddess, wife of the god of the ocean Aegir, uses a net to drown men

ransom: a sum of money demanded as payment for someone's life

Ratatosk: the squirrel that runs up and down the branches of Yggdrasill

Regin: the son of Hreidmar, brother of Otter

rock-giants: the giants who live in the mountains

Roskva: the daughter of the farmer Egil, becomes Thor's servant. Thialfi's sister

runes: magic symbols, first learnt by Odin

safe conduct: the right to pass over a piece of land without being harmed

Saga: a goddess who drinks daily with Odin in her hall

sapling: a young tree

scree: the small loose rocks and stones that pile up on mountainsides

scythe: a wooden-handled tool with a large curved blade, used for cutting tall crops or grass

shift: a loose dress

Sigyn: Loki's faithful wife

sisal: a plant used to make rope or twine

Skidbladnir: a magical collapsible ship that can hold all the gods and goddesses, made for Freyr by the dwarfs Son One and Son Two

Skirnir: Freyr's shining messenger

Skoll: the wolf that pursues the Sun and will swallow it before Ragnarok

sky-shoes: Loki's special shoes that let him run through the sky

Sleipnir: an eight-legged colt, the fastest horse in the nine worlds, given by Loki to Odin

sloe: the fruit of the blackthorn bush

solstice: the longest and shortest days in the year, when the Sun is furthest from the equator

spittoon: a container used to spit in

staff: a big stick

stallion: a male horse

steer: a young ox

stockade: a defensive fence built from tall upright wooden posts

stronghold: a fortified place of defence

Surt: the giant who guards Muspell, the realm of fire

tackle: the lines and pole used for fishing

Thialfi: the son of the farmer Egil, becomes Thor's servant, a fast runner

Thrud: Thor's daughter, promised to the dwarf Alvis

Thrym: the frost-giant who steals Thor's hammer

trencher: a wooden platter used for serving food

twine: a strong string

Tyr: Odin's brave son, god of battle, sacrifices his right hand

urchin: a dirty, raggedly dressed child

Utgard: the fortress of the Giant King

Valaskjalf: one of Odin's halls

Valhalla: Odin's massive hall with five hundred and forty doors, home to the fallen warriors chosen by the Valkyries

Vali: son of Loki and Sigyn, turned by the gods into a wolf, kills his own brother Narfi

Vali: son of Odin and his giant mistress Rind, survives Ragnarok

Valkyries: beautiful young women who bring dead warriors to Odin's hall Valhalla

Ve: brother of Odin and Vili

Vidar: the son of Odin and Grid who will avenge Odin's death

Vili: brother of Odin and Ve

wager: a bet

Warrior Gods: a group of gods, also known as the Aesir, associated with fighting and violence, including Odin, Thor and Tyr

Well of Mimir: well of wisdom, under one root of Yggdrasill

Well of Urd: home of the Three Norns

whetstone: a stone used to sharpen blades

Yggdrasill: an ash tree that links the nine worlds, known as the World Tree or the Guardian Tree

Ymir: the first giant, made of fire and ice. The nine worlds are formed from his body.

yoke: the wooden neck-frame used to couple oxen when they are ploughing

ACKNOWLEDGEMENTS

After the fire, the ashes and dust, Life and Life-to-be will sip dew and bear children, and their children will bear children.

One summer, long ago, my two young sons and I camped in Iceland, and the magical weeks we spent there among geysers and glaciers and volcanoes changed my life. I gave up my job as a publisher and, prompted by a great poet, set to work on retelling for adults the myths of the Norsemen. I taught school and college students in England and the USA about them, and wrote articles about how the Vikings and their literature should form part of our school syllabus. Then I used the myths to underpin my two young adult novels about Solveig, a Viking girl who travels to Constantinople in search of her father.

"But what you must do now," my friend Kate Agnew told me four years ago, "is to write a completely new version of these amazing myths for children, and invite Walker to publish it."

Along the way, an alphabet of friends and colleagues have encouraged and enabled me, among them Twiggy Bigwood and Tom Birkett and Marilyn Brocklehurst and Karen Clarke and Lynda Edwardes-Evans and Neil Gaiman and Bernard Hughes and Judith Jesch and Mari Siemon and Mary Steele and Eva Thengilsdottir and Will Wareing and Sern Watt. To them, and to my attentive and discerning agent Hilary Delamere; to my quite wonderful editor Denise Johnstone-Burt, the likes of whom I thought no longer existed, so alive to word, nuance and shape; to her spirited and meticulous assistant Daisy Jellicoe (who prepared the glossary); and to Walker's remarkable art editor Ben Norland; and to my loving half-Norwegian wife Linda, always ready to think through, and tease out, my sincere thanks.

All of these people then – because writing and putting together a book such as this involves a whole team – and also Jeffrey Alan Love! Hugely imaginative and forceful, sometimes witty, sometimes lyrical, often terrifying, his brilliant illustrations are true to the spirit and voice of the myths. You might think he was born to illustrate this book. That's what Walker thought, and so it has come to be...

First published 2017 by Walker Books Ltd, 87 Vauxhall Walk, London SE11 5HJ • 4 5 6 7 8 9 10 • Text © 2017 Kevin Crossley-Holland • Illustrations © 2017 Jeffrey Alan Love • The right of Kevin Crossley-Holland and Jeffrey Alan Love to be identified as author and illustrator respectively of this work has been asserted by them in accordance with the Copyright, Designs and Patents Act 1988 • This book has been typeset in Joanna • Printed and bound in China • All rights reserved. No part of this book may be reproduced, transmitted or stored in an information retrieval system in any form or by any means, graphic, electronic or mechanical, including photocopying, taping and recording, without prior written permission from the publisher. • British Library Cataloguing in Publication Data: a catalogue record for this book is available from the British Library • ISBN 978-1-4063-6184-1 • www.walker.co.uk